THE SOLAR-POWERED
SOUTHERN BELLE

The Solar-Powered Southern Belle

Short Stories

by

DONALD SECREAST

Adelaide Books
New York / Lisbon
2020

THE SOLAR-POWERED SOUTHERN BELLE
short stories
By Donald Secreast

Published by Adelaide Books, New York / Lisbon
adelaidebooks.org

Editor-in-Chief
Stevan V. Nikolic

For any information, please address Adelaide Books
at info@adelaidebooks.org
or write to:
Adelaide Books
244 Fifth Ave. Suite D27
New York, NY, 10001

ISBN: 978-1-952570-58-2

Printed in the United States of America

Contents

Woman in the Wind

Seventy-five miles from the coast—at least the coast that Patsy Shumaker was driving toward—the wind was coarse and fretful. A country boy's fingers. If Patsy hadn't grown up on the coast and spent days and nights on the Rainbow Pier where her father once sold fishing gear, licenses, and souvenirs, she wouldn't have been suspicious of the wind that molded her flannel shirt against her chest when she stepped out of her back door in Chocowinity, North Carolina, at six-thirty in the morning.

Of course, the television had been telling everybody for the last five days about the hurricane meandering from the Caribbean toward the North Carolina coast. Patsy's husband, Boyd, had tried to talk her out of going to the Sea Oats Resort on Atlantic Beach where Patsy worked, checking the time-share condominium owners in and out. Where she'd been checking them in and out for ten years. Before that, she had cleaned rooms at the Holiday Inn at Atlantic Beach.

If she hadn't known from her own experience that the storm was whipping up into a bad one and if she hadn't had the television telling her this hurricane meant business, then the fact that Boyd was advising her to miss a day of work would have tipped her off that being close to the ocean was particularly dangerous today. Now, for the ten years that Patsy had worked at Sea Oats Resort, Boyd had been asking her to find work closer to home. But he'd never asked her to miss a day—unless the wind was hauling damage.

In the winter, she could drive the seventy-five miles in an hour and a half, but in the summer, she might take two hours to get to her job. Traffic was always worse in the summer. People were always more stupid in the summer.

Or maybe they were just more stupid when they were on vacation. Having grown up and worked most of her life around people who were on vacation, Patsy knew that you didn't have to be poor to be stupid. The people she had to deal with at the resort were, for the most part, pretty well-to-do. None of her friends in Chocowinity or in Atlantic Beach could afford to buy a week at the Sea Oats. Then again, none of her friends could see the point in "time sharing." Like most of the projects built up along the beach, time sharing was a way for someone else to make money.

The wind plowed across the flat farmland, the dark, re-claimed swamp soil only a shade or two lighter than the clouds that fought the light. Veteran that she was driving through this kind of blow, Patsy always found herself leaning to the left, her arms growing stiff from keeping the car in the lane. And she had to anticipate when the wind would gust, or when it would suddenly drop off, causing her to over steer.

This kind of weather made the road feel a lot curvier than it was on milder days—when it reminded Patsy of the flat lane of her life. Or maybe Boyd was right, and she had been driving her hundred and fifty mile trip for too long.

Then again, more often than not, her check from the re-sort was what kept the groceries in the cupboard and the gas-oline in her and Boyd's cars. Patsy squeezed the steering wheel of her Monte Carlo. It was eight years old with some serious rust problems on the fenders and the doors. Boyd had been promising to fix them for the last two years, but he kept telling Patsy the job would take him a week or two. She couldn't get along without her car for a week or two. Boyd might let her use his car for two or three days, but not for a week or two. Besides, another side of Patsy reminded her that a car that spent as much time in the salt air as her Monte Carlo would always have to carry a few pounds of rust. Every car her father owned broke down from rust.

To her left, which was east, Patsy could see a dark line that ran the length of the horizon. The surf would be three or four times rougher than usual with the storm coming in. Most of the time share folks had left Atlantic Beach yesterday when the police came by the resort and suggested that all of them would be better off a little further inland. As always, the first people to get going were the ones driving the Mercedes. Even though the resort had the dunes between it and the beach, the spray was blowing off the ocean like a light rain. The people with the Jeeps and the trucks and the teenage children thought maybe they'd try to weather it out.

Patsy enjoyed going around to these people's condos and telling them that if the winds got up to ninety miles an hour the town turned off the power. In order to seem as helpful as possible, Patsy suggested to the hurricane watchers that they should stock up on batteries, candles, food, and fresh water if they planned to time share through the hurricane. People didn't seem to take the storm seriously until Patsy warned them to stay away from the windows.

When the time sharers seemed especially stubborn, Patsy told them to keep watch out toward the ocean when the eye of the hurricane passed over. Because the eastern wall of the storm was always the worst, with much stronger cyclonic winds than the western wall or first half of the storm, if there was going to be a storm surge, it would come just before the eye of the storm finished passing over, shortly before the second half of the storm hit.

"Just look out toward the ocean." Patsy would point in the direction of the slate gray water, waves already running seven to ten feet high. "If you see what looks like a bank of fog rolling in, you'd better head for high ground. What you're seeing is the storm wave heading in. I've seen them come over that topmost dune with eight feet to spare." The dune that Patsy referred to was twenty-five feet high.

She was able to tell people about that storm wave with conviction because she had actually seen it. What she didn't tell people was that the main office of the resort did have its own small generator. Not that it would ever get used by Mark Clinevell or Sebastian Waugh, the two managers at Sea Oats Resort. Both of them had their Jaguars to worry about. During hurricane season, the security guards took turns each week being on call for hurricane duty. This week, the guard who was responsible for protecting the resort grounds from the hurri-cane was Skip Pennell.

Of all the security guards who worked for Sea Oats, Skip Pennell was about the best as far as Patsy was concerned. She knew how he felt about high winds and salt spray. Once Clinevell and Waugh left, Patsy knew where she'd be able to find Skip.

Earlier in the morning when Boyd had been trying to talk Patsy out of driving to Atlantic Beach with the storm rolling in, he had offered to let her help him build the plaster cast for the deer head he was supposed to be mounting. Long ago, Boyd had learned that Patsy didn't care for the bloody part of his taxidermy business. She had tried to be of help when he first decided to take over his uncle's shop. Boyd's uncle had insisted that Boyd first practice with birds and small mammals.

Patsy hadn't minded when Boyd skinned his projects. She'd cleaned a few squirrels and chickens in her life before marrying Boyd. As a child who practically lived on the Rainbow Pier, she had also done her share of cleaning fish. In fact, she had shown Boyd how to cut the membranes that held the hide to the flesh. She'd shown him how to sprinkle the borax on the meat to keep it dry so the blood wouldn't stain the skins. If they had been planning on eating the meat, she'd have told Boyd to use cornmeal instead of borax. What she couldn't take was little jobs like scraping the brains out with the brain spoon, or in the case of birds, Boyd had suggested that she use a bobby pin.

Instead of getting used to her husband's taxidermy over the years, Patsy found the whole business harder to tolerate than when Boyd was still taking lessons from his uncle, when he would set box traps out in the fields then bring home the rabbits, the weasels, the skunks, and the squirrels he had caught then drowned in the river. Then there were the birds—especially the pigeons he practiced on. His uncle had managed somehow to get a permit to buy chloroform. He had shown Boyd how to make a cone out of a newspaper then stuff a piece of cotton soaked in chloroform down in the point of the cone. All the taxidermy student had to do was wedge the bird's head down deep into the cone. In three to five minutes, the bird was ready to be stripped.

It was the taxidermy which had also affirmed for Patsy that her husband was a sneak. Oh, she had discovered that he was a liar about one year after they were married. Boyd had promised her that he'd do whatever he could to let her keep living on Atlantic Beach. She was happy in the trailer they rented even if it did cost more than a medium-sized house rented for ten miles inland.

Patsy was cleaning rooms at the Holiday Inn. Boyd worked for a paving company over in Morehead City. They had enough money to pay their bills and go over to the Sanitary Fish Market in Beaufort for supper once a week. And Patsy could spend two or three hours every evening on the pier where she grew up.

Then the paving jobs started getting scarce. At first when Boyd complained about being laid off for days at a time, Patsy didn't even think to tell him all he had to do was look for another kind of work. Back then, she was the fastest and the most thorough housekeeper at the Holiday Inn, stripping beds and sanitizing toilets like she was plugged in to the manager's deepest dreams of efficiency. In the evenings, she could catch enough fish from her old pier to give Boyd a big supper. She just assumed that if Boyd got hard up enough for work he could come and Holiday Inn with her. And the restaurants always needed people—some of the better ones even in the winter because the population around Morehead City was fond of seafood all year round.

Back then, when Boyd had all that empty time, Patsy admitted she should have pushed him harder to go to the community college. He was smart. He could have become an electrician. The Sea Oats Resort was always looking for a good electrician. Or a good plumber. The first time she suggested taking a class or two, though, Boyd had collapsed on their couch, covered his face with his arms, and emptied his lungs as if he'd been holding his breath all day.

"Me and school don't mix." Boyd kept his arms over his eyes. "School always put me on edge."

At the time, Boyd's confession had stung Patsy's throat with love for her man. She identified with his discomfort.

However, school didn't put her on edge so much as it tried to drain her. The first boy she dated was friends with an older boy who worked in a funeral home in Swansboro. This older boy had given them a tour one evening of the preparation room and during a graphic description of the embalming process had explained to Patsy how the body fluids were removed from the corpse. She hadn't been able to bear school past her junior year.

No one had begged her to stick around until she graduated. As uncomfortable as she was in school, she had never caused trouble. Even as a teenager, she had possessed a detachment, an oceanic calm that the most idealistic teacher did not dare to disturb—could not have disturbed. Patsy was so clearly a child of Atlantic Beach and the Rainbow Pier, teachers rightly assumed they could not reach her with promises of escaping to a better life. Undeniably, Patsy was already where she wanted to be and she already knew what she had to do to stay there. So she was left alone to fish from the pier and not do her homework.

As it turned out, the only person who didn't realize that Patsy had never entertained the idea of living anywhere else but on Atlantic Beach was her husband. When he had come home one Sunday night after visiting his taxidermy uncle up in Chocowinity and announced that Patsy needed to pack her valuables and climb into his truck—that they were moving to Chocowinity—she had been so numbed by the possibility of leaving the beach that she packed half of her clothes before she realized she needed to protest and protest strongly.

"Look, Patsy." Boyd absorbed Patsy's protest by hugging her. "We don't own anything here." He put his head on her shoulder, exposing his scrawny neck to her teeth—if she had been in the mood to spill his blood. "We never will. You know as good as anybody that this whole place belongs to rich people. And it gets that way more every day."

Like a stingray gliding through her resentment, the realization that Boyd was right prevented Patsy from throwing him out in the yard–which was also their driveway. Every month, a new sprawling motel or condominium complex claimed more of the beaches, more of the back streets where gray sagging houses once contained people who used to spend long evenings on the pier with her, more of the drab little trailer parks where people like Patsy and Boyd still didn't have to compete with polished foreign cars for parking space.

Before she officially let Boyd move her out of their trailer and up the road, seventy-five miles inland, Patsy did persuade him to let her continue working at the Atlantic Beach Holiday Inn. While he was learning the taxidermy trade from his uncle, Boyd also figured to be working part-time for a Chocowinity paving company. After about two years with Boyd working for the Chocowinity paving company, Patsy learned that between the unreliable demand for paving in and around Chocowinity and the rainy weather, Boyd's job was a lot more part-time than she had imagined. She'd made the uncomfortable move from housekeeping at the Holiday Inn to condo checker at Sea Oats Resort because the pay was better–it had to be–and the hours were longer.

Not that Boyd was ever idle. In those first three years of learning his uncle's business, Boyd was out collecting animals to practice on every chance he got. Yes, Patsy had admitted to herself, her husband had lied to her, tricked her into moving inland. Led her into marriage then moved her way back from the ocean.

Then she had found out he was a sneak. Taxidermy, Patsy soon became convinced, was a sneaky man's business. Taking the outside of a real animal and wrapping it around some-thing artificial and fake . . . plaster, excelsior, wood , plastic . . . scooping out the brains with a spoon or a bobby pin, working the eyeballs out and replacing them with marbles—it was the kind of operation Patsy always suspected that education had been working on her.

Still, it was her husband's chosen work, and Patsy knew she could stomach it, although she recalled nothing in their wedding vows specifically mentioned taxidermy. Broad-minded as she tried to be, Patsy did draw the line at land animals with scales. On the day Boyd's uncle suggested that he needed practice with snakes and reptiles, Patsy had laid down the limit. No snakes. No reptiles.

Because she got home late from work, Boyd had always been good, after talking her into moving to Chocowinity, about fixing supper for Patsy. But when he started insisting on fixing her breakfast as well, she had gotten suspicious. She could tell when a man was trying too hard. In the freezer of their refriger-ator, Patsy found three burlap bags. Two contained frozen snakes and one contained a large frog. Boyd had explained that the best way to kill snakes and other reptiles was to put them in a cloth sack and freeze them. As disturbed as she was to learn that Boyd had sneaked around and put snakes in her freezer, Patsy was more disturbed by the thought of all those Cokes she had drunk which had been chilled by ice cubes covered by snakes.

Just north of New Bern, the halfway point in Patsy's drive to work, she came to Mize's Marine Supply. For people who expected the most modern line of marine supplies, Feldon Mize's store were a large disappointment. What he considered the fundamental fishing supplies was listed in large letters on a four by six foot wooden sign at the edge of the road in front of his store: BLOODWORMS AND CIGARETTES.

The building was old—wooden. Feldon and his wife lived upstairs. They were also old. Long ago, Feldon had lost interest in pleasing the deep sea fishermen who drove by his place. His inventory had shrunk along with his interest. More for his own convenience than for any desire to satisfy potential customers, Feldon did keep a few shelves pretty well stocked with basic groceries. As he had once explained to Patsy, as long as he ran a store, he got his own groceries delivered on a regular basis. For ten years, Patsy had been stopping in at Feldon's store twice a day. He sold K&K fried pies—the same kind of fried pies Patsy's father sold when he worked at the Rainbow Pier, and they had been her favorite food back then.

Not too long after her father died, the owners of the pier had stopped carrying the K&K brand of fried pies. For years, Patsy had looked for those particular pies, but not until she stopped one morning at Mize's Marine Supply did she find them. As it turned out, K&K was Feldon Mize's favorite pie maker as well, and when he saw how excited Patsy was about being reunited with the pastry, he counted her as a close friend.

Patsy always parked her Monte Carlo at the far corner of the building so she could walk across Feldon's parking lot. Long ago, the store must have done a thriving business because the entire parking lot was paved with bottle caps. Most of them were brown with age, but they still crunched when Patsy stepped on them. The sound reminded her of small shells being ground together, but the sound also carried a sight with it: people sitting around in the cooler evening air, Cokes, Pepsis, Nehis, and RC's sweating in their hands. They were the same kind of people who once fished from the Rainbow Pier in the evening. Mostly men who'd get off from work and drive down in the evening to sit in the breeze, hoping to take home a few fish for supper or breakfast.

Once inside Feldon Mize's store, the customer had to cross about fifteen feet of empty space before reaching the shelves where the stock was watched over by an old man molded to a wooden rocking chair. Feldon had pulled all of his shelves and glass-front counters in a circle around his wood-burning stove. Beside his rocking chair, Feldon had a table he'd bought at a state school inventory sale. The table was about six feet long and two and a half feet high. Feldon kept his cash register on this table at one end. The remaining space he used for his check out counter. While he wouldn't hesitate to crawl out of his chair to help a customer select the bloodworms he needed, Feldon saw no sense in his having to move from his chair to ring up somebody's crackers and sardines.

Although Feldon didn't advertise them on his big sign outside, he also kept crickets in an old drink box back in a dark corner of the store. Patsy suspected that Feldon kept them for company because they chirped constantly, and it was a sound that inexplicably reminded Patsy of the ocean—of surf and seagulls, of the privacy she used to feel when she fished from the very end of the pier on a late autumn or early spring evening.

When Patsy reached the circle of shelves illuminated by the two fluorescent lights that Feldon referred to as his "fixtures," the old man waved to her without detaching his elbow from the armrest of his chair.

"Lord, girl. Don't tell me you're driving to work with this storm slapping in." Feldon leaned forward in his chair and locked his fingers together.

"Noooo." Patsy unbuttoned the sleeves of her flannel shirt and pushed them up over her elbows. Feldon always kept the center of the store warmer than Patsy could bear. "I just drove down here so I could get my fried pies."

"I'd judge it's highly windy even to go out for fried pies." Feldon laughed.

"If I'd been thinking, I could have picked up my supply when I stopped here last night." Patsy walked over to the K&K shelf and picked up a pie. A particularly strong gust of wind rattled the windows. Taking the disturbance as a suggestion, Patsy picked up seven pies, five apple and two cherry.

As he rang up Patsy's purchase, Feldon shook his head. "People down on Atlantic Beach are boarding up windows, tying down shrubbery, waterproofing doors, evacuating pets—and here you are buying fried pies."

"I'm experienced with hurricanes." Patsy reached underneath Feldon's table and pulled out a small paper bag.

"Unless you rode the storm of thirty-eight, you've not experienced a hurricane." Feldon took Patsy's money, dug her change out of the cash register, and handed it back to her without taking his eyes from her face.

At least three times a year during hurricane season, Feldon reminded Patsy of the storm of thirty-eight. "September twenty-first. My uncle had moved his family up North to Long Island, Westhampton Beach. My daddy and me had gone up with them to help them unload their furniture. Course, the storm made us have to sit out most of the day. The weather bureau down in Florida had announced that the big hurricane that scraped the North Carolina coast had turned out to sea and wouldn't be bothering any American citizens no more. So when the bad weather crowded up around Long Island, we thought it was just some left over wind from that hurricane that wasn't going to bother anybody."

In response to Patsy rolling down the top of her paper bag, Feldon leaned his elbow on his school table. "I was pretty young then, so I couldn't really carry any of the big pieces. But around three o'clock, when we thought the weather had finally calmed down, I was walking from the truck to the house with a leather footstool in my arms when out of nowhere this wall of water folded down over me."

Feldon stroked his eyebrow and gazed past Patsy. "I didn't even feel the water coming down. Just got all sense knocked out of me. And when I come to, I was hanging from the cross bar of a telephone pole, thirty feet off the ground. The ocean was just a couple of feet below my face. There floating by was one of my uncle's rubber boots. He'd just bought them the day before, and I'd wanted a pair so bad because they were black with a white sole. I'd never seen a two-toned rubber boot back then."

All Patsy could do was nod and roll the top of her paper bag even tighter while leaning toward the door. She still had thirty-five miles to drive, and she knew what came next.

"Before I could even wonder what had happened to my daddy and my uncle and his family, another big wave roared over me. And this time when I woke up, I was on the roof of my uncle's house, floating in Quantuck Bay, and all the rest of my family was on the roof with me. My aunt was clutching my cousin in one arm and that leather stool in the other arm." Feldon held his elbows out from his body to clarify for Patsy what his aunt looked like.

"You can bet I couldn't get home fast enough, and I've never been back to Long Island since and know I'm as close to the ocean as I'll ever want to be again." Feldon shifted in his rocking chair and hooked one elbow over the back of the chair. "Six hundred and fifty people died in the storm of thirty-eight. But I wasn't one of 'em. Made me a religious man."

"Something would be bad wrong with you if it didn't." Patsy leaned across the counter and gave Feldon's chair a push.

The old man just let himself rock with his arm still cocked over the chair's back.

Crossing the long, arched bridge which connected Morehead City to Atlantic Beach, Patsy felt the unobstructed power of the wind for the first time. It was now coming head on. She had to keep the accelerator pushed halfway down just to travel twenty-five miles an hour. Large drops of rain splatted against her windshield. What really held Patsy's attention was the total lack of traffic. She'd seen maybe three cars as she drove through Morehead City, but except for her, the whole length of the bridge was empty. The emptiness reminded Patsy of Feldon's story. She knew he told it to her as a warning. She appreciated his concern, but she'd heard it too many times. An old warning was an empty warning. Talk as much as he might about the storm of `38, it no longer had the wind in it.

On the other side of the bridge, Patsy turned right, driving parallel to the ocean. She now leaned even harder against her door, grateful for the dunes and the three blocks of buildings which broke up the wind. Soon, she could tell, the winds would shift, coming in almost parallel to the beach. That shift would let her know when the hurricane was arriving–when the wind stopped coming from the east and began curving from north to south. Then there'd come the eye of the storm. After that, the wind would pick up again but blowing from west to east curving up from south to north. That big shift in the middle of the storm was what caused so much damage. All the buildings and trees that had managed to brace themselves against the first half of the storm usually weren't able to tolerate the blow coming from the opposite direction. Only what could bend both ways and be flattened without breaking was what survived a hurricane.

Passing through the gates of the Sea Oats Resort, Patsy slowed down and scrutinized the security guard station, a large booth whose windows had been covered with plywood sheets braced by two-by-fours and reinforced with sandbags. A slot about two feet long and one foot wide had been cut in one plywood sheet. Patsy thought she saw Skip Pennell inside the booth. His face was so pale, he almost glowed in the dark. Easing up as close to the door of the guard station as she could get, Patsy motioned for Skip to come out.

With his arms wrapped around his head, Skip lunged out of the guard station, paused to open the car door, then flipped himself onto the seat beside Patsy. She thought Skip wore too much cologne for a security guard, but he had assured her when he first came to work for the resort that he took this job to help pay for his way through the community college where he was studying landscaping.

"I'm going deaf out here, Patsy!" Skip patted his ears. His hair looked as if he'd used an electric mixer for a pillow, and he had a glittering coat of sand all over his face and neck.

"Little drafty in that booth, is it?" Patsy leaned against her door to inspect Skip. His clothes were twisted like those belonging to a man who'd been hearing strange noises all around him.

"It's going to get worse, ain't it, Patsy?" Skip noticed his wristwatch was turned the wrong way. He adjusted it then tuned his shirt cuffs then his sleeves.

"This is just what they call the peripheral wind, Skip. This is the air that's trying to get away from the real wind." Patsy leaned over her steering wheel and studied the guard booth. "Does that little house feel safe to you?"

"About as safe as anything else on this island." Skip followed Patsy's stare. "It's been reinforced. Mr. Clinevell and Mr. Waugh said it looked safe to them."

For a few more seconds, Patsy studied Skip's shelter. "In about fifteen minutes, you'll be watching the rear ends of Mr. Clinevell's and Mr. Waugh's Jaguars as they strike out for the heart of the continent." Patsy leaned further over her steering wheel and turned her face toward the sky. "Skip, you'll know the hurricane's here when big things start falling. And that utility pole right over there is a prime candidate for coming down."

Skip crouched down and followed Patsy's finger. "It could come down right across the guard station." He knew he had a good eye for measurements.

"People who don't hang around for the hurricane don't usually think about power poles falling down, but they always do. Wood poles just don't have much of a chance against one-hundred-fifty-mile-an-hour winds. Especially when them poles are planted in sand." Patsy clicked her tongue and leaned back.

"But them poles are braced." Skip kept staring at the utility pole.

"The braces are as much in the sand as the poles are, Skip." Patsy kept her voice quiet. She wanted Skip to have trouble hearing her above the wind.

Skip leaned further over the dashboard, following the swaying power lines. "I've a good notion just to quit while I still have time to get home without having to swim."

"Hang on for a while longer." Patsy tapped her chin as she pretended to calculate just how much more wind that power line could tolerate. "I might be able to help you."

"I don't see why I have to stay here when Clinevell and Waugh get to leave."

"You're the security guard, Skip." Resting her elbow on her steering wheel, Patsy turned to face the young man. "Clinevell and Waugh hired you so they wouldn't have to ride out this kind of weather."

As if he'd just come to an important decision, Skip puffed out his cheeks and nodded his head once. "Then I ought to just go ahead and quit right now and show C&W the way across that bridge into Morehead City."

"So you're determined not to stay?" Patsy allowed herself to slump and dropped her gaze to the space between her and Skip.

"I'm going straight from your car to mine." Skip's voice slid up in pitch as a gust of wind shook Patsy's heavy car.

"How much money you got on you?" Patsy glanced toward the clubhouse building where she knew the managers were waiting for her.

"Why?"

"You give me fifty dollars, and I'll be the security guard during this hurricane." Patsy kept her eyes set on the clubhouse. She didn't like to lie except when she was facing hurricanes. This was perhaps the reason she could forgive Boyd's sneakiness in wanting to be a taxidermist.

For a few seconds, Skip stared at the clubhouse. "You want to stay out here with the storm?"

"I grew up with storms. What I want is your fifty dollars." Patsy smiled and held out her hand, palm up.

After a brief struggle, Skip pulled out his wallet. "All I've got on me is thirty dollars . . ."

Patsy wiggled her fingers. "You can owe me the twenty. But don't leave until Clinevell and Waugh take off. I promise, you won't have to wait more than ten minutes once I get inside the clubhouse. Hang around just long enough to wave bye to them."

As Patsy expected, the two managers were waiting for her, practically standing by the door with their overnight bags.

Except for the steady hum of the wind, the clubhouse was unnaturally quiet. Usually, the jukebox in the game room was belting out music, drowning out even the noises of the pinball machines and video games. Patsy enjoyed pinball. The Rainbow Pier had three machines which she mastered by the time she was twelve. What she didn't like was the way all the arcade games along the boardwalk had been replaced by video games. But the Sea Oats Resort had to satisfy everyone's taste for amusement.

"How's Skip holding up?" Mark Clinevell didn't look up from the fat ring of keys he was checking.

"He'll be okay." Patsy took the keys from Clinevell and walked behind the counter that was usually covered with brochures. At least the two managers had tidied up the place. Patsy suspected that their type was usually most meticulous when they were nervous. If they'd been the big slow types who dragged deer, bobcats, foxes, and an occasional alligator into Boyd's taxidermy shop, Patsy knew she'd have more trouble. Clinevell and Waugh were so slick, they often slid off themselves.

"Keep an eye on him, Patsy." Sebastian Waugh picked up his bag and stood beside the door. "You've got one family over in J-thirty-five. Everybody else decided to evacuate."

"I'll go check on them. Let them know where to come if they have any trouble." Patsy picked up her clipboard but left her walkie-talkie on the shelf under the counter. Except for Skip, who would be gone soon after the managers, she didn't have anybody to walkie talk to.

"We'll be back first thing tomorrow if the roads are passable." Clinevell gripped the door handle but leaned away from the door, as if to give Patsy one last chance to change her mind.

"If you hang around much longer, the sand in the wind is going to start pitting your paint jobs." Patsy knew where both men had their values anchored.

Jostling his bag to test his grip, Sebastian Waugh studied how much weather was blowing between him and his car. "Mark and I really appreciate your watching the office for us while we're gone."

Mark Clinevell nodded. "It's a valuable service."

Waugh leaned across the counter and pressed a fifty dollar bill into Patsy's hand. "Don't take any unnecessary chances."

Clinevell opened the door, admitting a gust of wind which pushed him back into Waugh. Both men leaned forward and bolted for their cars. As soon as they had disappeared around the gates at the entrance to the resort, Patsy saw Skip Pennell run from the guard station and climb into his Chevette.

With her bag of fried applied pies balanced on her clipboard, Patsy hurried to the back of the clubhouse, past the game room, past the hot tub, past the salesroom, back to the employee lounge where she stored her pies in her locker and removed a second clipboard and her plastic bracelet machine. Before the wind changed direction, she had to pay a visit to the family in unit J-thirty-five.

Sand and spray stinging her face, Patsy crouched as she ran in a slant against the wind. Although still coming from the east, the wind had picked up velocity, almost as dense as a warning. Still, Patsy knew the hurricane needed more time to arrive because she could still hear the waves. When the hurricane winds arrived, all other sounds disappeared.

J-thirty-five was a nice condo—third floor, facing the ocean. Shielding her face with her two clipboards, Patsy saw that the waves were easily ten feet high now. Several of the shingles on top of the resort's gazebo down on the first row of dunes were already beginning to come loose. To Patsy, the wind pushing her away from the condo's balcony didn't feel like one solid flow. She could distinguish layers and rhythms;

a flat palm pushed against her forehead while a swirl wrapped around her ear—a crescent grazed her cheek as a flounder of wind flopped down her chest and slipped off her stomach. Eels vibrated around her legs.

From the length of time it took for someone to start opening the door, Patsy knew she had gotten J-thirty-five's occupants out of bed. This knowledge cheered her. People who thought they could sleep late on the day a hurricane was scheduled to arrive didn't really appreciate what was headed toward them. Had these people met her at the door, wearing their warm clothes and waterproof shoes, Patsy would have been less confident in what she was about to do.

The man who opened the door was lean, with dark hair on his bony chest. All he wore was a pair of nylon running shorts. At first, he seemed about to challenge Patsy for disturbing him so early in the morning, but the wind blew his objections off his face.

"Sorry to disturb you." Patsy held up her regulation clipboard which held her i.d. card.

"I've already told the manager that we don't plan to leave." The man twisted sideways so the wind wasn't blasting flat against his chest and stomach. He crouched slightly.

"I understand." Patsy also twisted slightly so more wind could get to the time-sharer. "I just need to do a quick inventory and get you to sign a couple of consent forms."

Drifting behind the door he held open, the man motioned Patsy to come in. "Consent forms?"

"In extreme situations, when a resort member wants to exert his rights, the company wants to protect its butt." Patsy took her time coming in far enough so the man could close the door. Late September was one of the less expensive rental periods, so she didn't feel she had to be especially shrewd with this man. People who came this time of the year had been sucked in by one of the resort's salesmen.

With a decisive twist of her wrist, Patsy flipped a clipboard in front of the man's bare chest. "Just look over these waivers. The top one releases the Sea Oats Resort from any liability in the event you or any of the members of your party are killed." Halfway through Patsy's sentence, a woman wandered from the back bedroom, pulling a terry cloth beach robe around her.

"Lathan, what's wrong?" The woman sounded more sleepy than alarmed.

Not waiting for Lathan to answer, Patsy pointed to the sheet of paper beneath the first sheet. "And the second form releases the resort from any liability for any injuries you and your party might receive because of the storm."

As he signed the two forms, the man glanced at the woman. "This is standard with all these places, Becky." He handed Patsy the clipboard and stepped toward the door. "I bet you've spent most of the morning getting people to sign those forms."

Ignoring the man's move toward the door, Patsy stepped sideways into the condo's kitchen. "No. You're the only guests left in the whole resort." Patsy placed the clipboard with the waivers on the counter next to where Becky was standing. Then she began to check the inventory in the kitchen.

"Aren't you supposed to wait until we check out to do that?" The man took a stiff step to the door and grabbed the doorknob.

"This is standard procedure." Patsy opened the top cupboard doors and checked off the contents on her sheet. When she got to the shelf holding the popcorn popper, she leaned against the counter. "I'm also supposed to warn you about going out after the storm passes. Sometimes we do have what the coast guard calls delayed storm surges, big waves that come in an hour or two after the hurricane's over. The beach should be avoided. A lot of sand shifting takes place, and you could step on some unstable ground. And you'd have to worry about beached jellyfish, dislocated rats and snakes. Keep a sharp eye out for downed electrical wires."

"Are we likely to lose power?" The woman sat down on a stool on the other side of the counter from Patsy.

"One way or another, the power's going out." Patsy resumed taking the inventory. "The town cuts the power off when the wind hits ninety miles an hour—just as a safety precaution. Lots of times, a tree or a billboard will take lines down before the wind gets up to ninety miles an hour. If the wind gets really hard, it's going to take lines down all over the place."

"So if we lose power, we could be without it for quite a while?" The woman no longer sounded alarmed.

"Depending on the amount of damage, how many poles are down, how many lines are cut or buried." Patsy finished her inventory. "I've known the power boys to get everything restored in three days, but I've also seen them take a week to get the juice flowing."

"Water'll be off too, I suppose?" The woman was no longer looking at Patsy but at Lathan, who was still standing in front of the door with his arms crossed.

"Even if it's coming out of the pipes, don't drink it because you can be sure the treatment plant is going to be out of operation for as long as the power's off." Patsy reached inside her slicker's oversized pocket where she was carrying the bracelet machine."

Lathan shook his head and moved to the end of the counter where he leaned in Becky's direction. "We have twelve gallon milk jugs full of spare water and another six gallons of Evian."

"That should hold you fine." Patsy smiled. "I mean it's not like you're going to be trapped on this island for a month. The roads will be clear in a day or two, and the restaurants over in Morehead City will be open for business tomorrow or the next day."

The man straightened up from the counter. "That's what I've been telling Becky since we decided to meet this hurricane head on."

"One more request." Patsy pulled the bracelet machine out of her pocket. "The Coast Guard asked us to get all of the hurricane watchers to wear one of these."

"What's that?" The woman leaned across the counter where Patsy was centering the first plastic bracelet in the slot.

"You know them bracelets they give you at the hospital?" Patsy handed the woman a small rectangle of paper. "Write your full name and address on this."

As soon as the woman finished, Patsy slid another small rectangle of paper toward her. "Would you write his full name and address on this one?"

While the woman wrote, Patsy took the first piece of paper and inserted it inside a small plastic pocket in the bracelet. By pulling down on a small lever, Patsy sealed the label inside the plastic bracelet. She repeated the operation for the man's bracelet.

By this time, Lathan had sat down beside Becky. "What's the Coast Guard got to do with bracelets?"

"In case you get washed away somewhere, the bracelets make it easier for them to identify your body." Patsy flipped the machine around and pulled out a device that resembled the head of a small adjustable wrench. "Hold your bracelet right there." Patsy tapped her finger on the top of the envelope holding the woman's name and address." Patsy noticed the last name was different from the man's. "I have to special latch it." She screwed the jaws of the wrench tightly down on the band of the bracelet. "A good storm surge wave can tear the clothes right off a person." As she attached the man's bracelet, Patsy saw out of the corner of her eye that the woman was sitting very quietly, staring at her bracelet.

Within an hour after Patsy returned to the clubhouse, she saw Lathan and Becky, in a Cherokee Chief, leaving the resort. Patsy checked the shutters around the clubhouse then locked all the doors. Back in the Jacuzzi room, she'd left a triple row of windows unshuttered. Keeping her eyes on the clouds tumbling in from the ocean, Patsy undressed and stepped into the Jacuzzi. Close by, she had set a tray with four fried pies and a thermos jug of hot coffee.

Even before she got married, it had been hard to get alone with hurricanes—even tropical storms for that matter. She'd been ten in 1968 when Hurricane Gladys had skirted the coast. Her father thought she had gone inland with her mother, but Patsy had sneaked back to the Rainbow Pier and watched the storm roar by from there. Then in seventy-one, Doria had come through. She had been a tropical storm instead of a hurricane, but she came right across the coast scary enough to sink deep into Patsy's heart. She'd been on the pier for Doria. That was where Patsy had watched Agnes and Bret as well as Dennis. None of the names ever fit the storms. But Gloria, in 1985, had been the best. This clubhouse hadn't been built then, so Patsy had met the storm over in condo A-thirty-eight, the unit closest to the ocean. At times, Patsy thought the whole building was going to blow down, a sensation that distracted her from the storm. Then when it was over, both stairways had been ripped from the building, and she had to wait until the power company came over with a crane.

She'd learned her lesson. What she might lose in view, she could make up in comfort. She settled more deeply into the Jacuzzi. Soon, the private generator would have to kick on. The winds had to be hitting the ninety-mile mark. And the clouds were beginning to take on that green glow, letting Patsy know the hurricane had arrived. So much sand and spray were dashing around outside that Patsy could see the currents of the wind moving like gigantic stingrays, and if she stepped outside now, she'd be swept away in an embrace that would leave her smelling like the ocean.

Bear Season

Officially, the Cherokee Trading Post didn't open until nine o'clock. However, for the two weeks that Taft Scott had been in charge of opening the souvenir stand, he'd been unlocking the cyclone fence that enclosed the front parking lot no later than seven o'clock. He moved a lot slower than the trading post's owner, Lloyd Redwine, who was in the hospital, and Taft had more trouble than he expected in arranging the outdoor merchandise: the fancy bedspreads had to be hung from the clothesline which stretched from one corner porch post to a post stuck halfway between the porch and the fence; the eight life-size hillbilly dolls had to be propped up in the rocking chairs which sold separately from the dolls; the wooden yard ornaments and whirligigs had to be balanced in the hollow log umbrella stands; the miniature and not-so miniature totem poles which could serve as mailbox posts had to be arranged according to size.

But the job which Taft hated the most—consequently, the job he always performed first—was dragging Lloyd Redwine's main tourist attraction off the porch where it spent the night covered by a heavy tarp, and across the gravel parking lot to a spot right beside the narrow mountain road, but not so close to the pavement that it might be accidentally knocked down by some flatland driver who wasn't used to the stubbornness of the mountain curves.

Years ago, if a souvenir stand had any hopes of surviving, it had to have attractions other than the merchandise it sold. Taft remembered driving down to the ocean and stopping at souvenir stands that had alligators and monkeys and exotic birds. His favorite had always been peacocks. He knew they were just glorified chickens, and he'd raised enough chickens in his life to know better than to be impressed with them, but he'd never been able to fully explain to himself where the peacock had come up with an idea like that tail of his. Most of the stores sold the feathers. More than once, Taft had spent money he should have kept in his pocket on a bouquet of peacock tail feathers.

Souvenir stands didn't keep animals like they used to. Probably for the best, Taft admitted. The biggest part of the animals he used to stare at through the chicken wire fences didn't look healthy. He'd raised enough animals to know when they weren't being taken care of. You couldn't help but smell the neglect even if you didn't want to see it.

So now, most souvenir stand owners just hoped their displays of cement bird baths and yard animals, their bright quilts, their wall-size tapestries of tigers chasing down curly-horned deer would pull in the tourists. Other souvenir stand owners went a step further and put up large signs with a hillbilly couple inviting folks to come in and browse. Then, there were men who went a step further and invested in genuine objects of interest: fifteen foot totem poles, wigwams big enough to seat twenty people at a time, arrows with their shafts made out of telephone poles, giant plaster horses, and huge wooden Indians with elaborately carved feather headdresses.

But Lloyd Redwine hadn't been satisfied with what other souvenir stands used as attractions. He'd wanted something to put in front of his store that would draw people in and keep them thinking about his place long after they'd left. Somewhere, he'd purchased a nine-foot grizzly bear.

As far back as he could remember, Taft had never been especially fond of stuffed animals. Something about them was too unnatural. And the bigger they got, the more unnatural they looked to Taft. At least with a stuffed owl or squirrel, you could ignore it. Just turn your back to it and forget it. A nine-foot bear was different. Even with your back turned to it, some part of the animal stuck out in the corner of your eye or over the top of your head.

For the five years Lloyd Redwine had been running the Cherokee Trading Post with his grizzly bear looming over the road beside the trading post, Taft had kept his distance from the animal. Of course, for the first three years the store was open, Taft didn't spend that much time around the place except in the early fall when he and his wife set up a small stand in the corner of the trading post parking lot where they sold apple cider. For the rest of the year, he had his job in the lumber yard of Hibriten Furniture Factory to drive to every day. Besides, everybody who lived in Goshen Hollow knew that most of what Lloyd Redwine sold was junk for the tourists.

Then, two years ago when Taft retired, he'd found himself spending more time at the Cherokee Trading Post. At church one morning, Lloyd had asked Taft if he could use some part-time work. He'd helped Lloyd arrange cement bird baths and relocate the larger yard animals. As strong as Lloyd was, he still needed help with the life-size cement deer. Taft had never thought about how a man had to rotate his cement animal stock just like a grocer had to rotate his dairy products.

Reluctant as he was to be taught, Taft even let himself learn to use the cash register. Some afternoons, he'd come to the trading post after wrestling with his tiller all morning, getting the garden chewed up so his wife could plant them a little vegetable garden, and with his hands still tingling from the tractor's convulsions, he'd sweat more in an hour over that cash register than he'd done behind his tiller in five hours.

No job he'd ever done—in the lumber yard, on the farm, or in the trading post—was as hard for Taft as wrestling that grizzly bear off the porch and across the parking lot. First of all, the bear was heavier than life itself. Lloyd swore that the bear was stuffed mostly with straw. Finally, just the other night, when Taft was visiting Lloyd in the hospital, Taft had forced Lloyd to admit that the straw was stacked around an iron skeleton, and attached to the skeleton was a fair amount of reinforced heavy-gauge chicken wire. Besides, the hide of a nine-foot grizzly bear weighed more than a hundred pounds.

Lloyd made a big noise about how the bear was mounted on its platform with ball bearing casters. And maybe those casters were Cadillac fine when the bear was skating across the slick floor of some big city hotel—which is where Lloyd hinted he'd found his tourist attraction—but that first morning when Taft tried to drag the bear across that gravel parking lot, he thought he was going to be crushed or shredded by the bear at least twenty times before he finally stumbled with it up beside the road. That little job had taken him an hour and forty-five minutes and at least a half pint of blood from the scrapes he got when the claws either raked his shoulders or the top of his head. All he could be grateful for was the fact that no tourists had driven by or pulled in while he was struggling with the bear. Taft could endure being mauled by a stuffed bear. He'd been kicked by cows and horses—even his wife a few times.

He'd been poked by rough lumber, fallen off hacks, and cut by every kind of blade made by man. But he couldn't bear the idea of strangers seeing him hugging a large dead animal that didn't even belong in the Blue Ridge Mountains.

After that first morning, Taft had spent the rest of the day trying to figure out an easier way to get the bear back to its nightly resting place on the porch. Lloyd had never dared leave the bear close to the road—even though he could have kept it from being stolen just by sliding the bear back five feet so it'd be inside the cyclone fence. Too many boys liked to drive around at night shooting the road signs. Taft agreed with Lloyd that a nine-foot-high stuffed bear would be too much of a temptation for restless men looking for interesting targets.

From the trading post porch all the way up to the bear's place beside the road, Taft had laid two tracks of rough planks. While the bear didn't ride the wooden tracks very smoothly, occasionally twisting off into the gravel, Taft was able to cut the moving time down to a sweaty twenty or thirty minutes. The job might not have been as hot if he didn't wear one of Lloyd's heavy denim jackets, but no matter how carefully he worked, the bear continued to scrape him with its claws. To protect his head, Taft had dug up an old army helmet liner—glad for once that Cora never threw anything away. Years ago, his boy, Eston, had played army in the helmet liner which Taft now wore strapped on his head. He still had a line of scabs where the bear's claws had furrowed the top of his scalp.

From what Taft had gathered from Lloyd's wife, Jeanette, and from the way Lloyd looked stretched out in intensive care, he wouldn't be coming home anytime soon, much less returning to the trading post. That meant Taft would be wrestling the bear out to the road even when the mornings were a lot hotter than they were now in late April. Taft hated to think what he and the bear were going to smell like in July and August.

Every morning, he hated the bear all over again as soon as he pulled the tarp off of it. Taft didn't mind sweating as long as it had some point. As long as it was honest. But a grizzly bear in the Appalachian Mountains was a lie. It was a lie losing large patches of its fur. Taft had no idea how old the bear was. Back when Lloyd brought it from out west, the bear already had some serious creases in its hide where not only the fur was missing but where the skin resembled cardboard that had been folded over and over.

The arms hung too low; the paws drooped. Maybe if the bear hadn't slouched so much it would have been easier to move. Instead of looking like a wild beast about to attack, the bear looked more like it was offering itself up to the law after a lifelong chase, its arms stuck out resignedly as if waiting for the handcuffs to be attached. That attitude made Taft hate the bear even more.

Even the bear's snarl drooped. So much of the black paint and plaster on the bear's mouth had been chipped away that from a short distance, the bear looked as if it had been chewing gum only to have a bubble explode all over its muzzle. An upper and a lower fang were missing. About every six months, Lloyd got embarrassed enough by his bear to talk about having it remounted, but when the idea had first come to him and he'd found out that a remounting job would run right at seven or eight hundred dollars, Lloyd had confined his dissatisfaction to making plans rather than signing a contract. The point that Lloyd made, and it sounded perfectly reasonable to all of his neighbors, was that he couldn't see paying that kind of money just to stick it back out beside the road in all kinds of weather.

In this corner of Wilkes County, people held on to a car or a shack or a bear until it broke down. If it couldn't be patched up it would be left behind. Weeds would grow up around it, and one day, people would just stop seeing it. Not only the people who owned the piece of junk but the neighbors and the relatives as well. Once a tool or a place or even a person had all the use drained out of him, he turned invisible.

After Taft got the bear struggled into position, he leaned against it to catch his breath. From where he rested, looking up at the bear's muzzle, the mouth looked drawn up to the left, like a man who's got his cud of tobacco wedged crooked in his jaw. For a moment, Taft thought about finding one of the felt hillbilly hats that Lloyd used on his life-size dolls. One summer, he'd ordered a huge box of the floppy hats, all of them with a little sign glued to the front: my weak end hat. Then again, Lloyd might not think it was funny, putting a hat on his tourist attraction. Besides, Taft reminded himself, no grizzly could be a hillbilly bear.

Crossing the parking lot, Taft picked up the planks, a stack of six balanced on his shoulder. He remembered carrying the same kind of planks from one lumber hack to another on mornings just like this one. Thirty years in that lumber yard. He didn't miss it. Not the mud, not the cold, not the heat. If he missed anything, it was the way the seasons changed around the factory: when the blossoms on the trees along the factory's acres of fence first came out, then when the leaves first started unfolding in a green mist. The first touch of gold and scarlet at the end of the summer and then the day when he looked up from stacking and realized that the trees were empty. More than once, Taft had argued with the younger men he worked with about what a faded place Florida would have to be without any change in the seasons. Taft wasn't surprised that places like Las Vegas had to have gambling joints and California had to have Disneyland. The people had to have something to distract them from the lack of seasons.

As Taft stacked the lumber beside the trading post, he tried to keep from looking at the clearing just twenty feet away where he and Lloyd had been working. The wild cherry tree which had caused Lloyd's accident was now in full bloom, looking so pure that Taft couldn't help but feel guilty. He hadn't had a full night's sleep since Lloyd had been knocked off his ladder. When Taft closed his eyes, he could see the white nimbus of the cherry tree and the dark outline of the limb that Lloyd had just cut through.

A large car screeching around the curve reminded Taft that he still had the rest of the outdoor merchandise to set up before he could afford the luxury of guilt. This morning, Cora had offered to come and open the store for Taft. She told him that as irritable as he was with her—and all she'd done was scramble his eggs and pour his coffee for him—he'd be doing Lloyd more of a favor by staying at home and trying to catch up on his sleep instead of stomping around the trading post biting off the customers' heads. Taft had slipped into a fit of laughing when he imagined Cora and her blood clot knotted legs out in the gravel hugged up to that bear.

As always when taking a position against her husband's laughter, Cora pressed the knuckles of her left hand into the trough of her lower spine and held her other fist under Taft's nose. "I'd get the job done, mister. I'd get the job done."

And Taft knew that she would. If she had to blow out every artery in her body, she'd have moved the bear.

As sociable as Cora could be, both she and Taft knew that she wasn't really comfortable working around the public. Let somebody ask her directions, and she could keep them in their driveway for half a day, but like most of the people born and raised in Goshen Hollow, Cora was too shy and too independent to sell strangers the trash on display at the Cherokee Trading Post.

Unlocking the door to the trading post, Taft had to correct himself. Not all the merchandise Lloyd sold was trash. In another month, Cora would have five quilts ready to bring to the trading post. She'd been working on them all winter.

Then there were Taft's whips. About a year ago, the man who'd been supplying the trading post with whips went out of business. Neither Taft nor Lloyd had been surprised because five or six people had brought whips back for a refund. Usually, tourists never brought defective merchandise back. But one man had driven all the way back from Raleigh—about two hundred miles—because the whip he'd bought for his son had started coming unraveled after the boy had popped it three times.

So when Lloyd saw that the place where the whips hung was getting empty, he asked Taft to try and make some whips for him. Lloyd's cousin was a taxidermist who gave him a good price on rawhide strips, and Taft knew he could easily whittle the handles. He had taken one of the cheap whips home, planning to puzzle out how they were made. Before he had pulled out all of the tacks which held the leather to the handle, Cora had pointed out to him that the whip was nothing more than a triple braid tapering off to a normal braid with a final strand of rawhide sticking out far enough to latch on to whatever the whip slinger wanted to catch. With his wife's help, Taft was braiding anywhere from ten to fifteen whips a week, depending on whether the whips he was making were the baby whips, which were three feet long, the junior whips, which were six feet long, or the bullwhips, which were eight feet long.

Although he'd been selling his whips for a year now, Taft still felt excited when he saw tourists admiring his work. It was one thing to sell a gallon of apple cider that he and Cora had made. He'd been selling chickens and produce all of his life.

But it was something else to see people admiring something he'd spent a night pulling together. Men and women and children who climbed out of expensive cars and station wagons who talked with voices like cream rising to the top of a bucket of warm milk ran their fingers over his whips. Sometimes they shivered. Sometimes they fell into silence. Sometimes, they laughed, but Taft knew they were laughing at what they were thinking about the whips—not at the whips themselves. With the old whips, only the children were interested. The whips that Taft made interested everybody.

Then there was the money. The three-foot whips sold for twelve dollars. The six-foot whips sold for eighteen dollars, and the eight foot whips sold for twenty-five dollars. Of course, Lloyd got fifty percent because he provided the leather and the outlet.

The predominant smell of the trading post was a blend of red cedar and leather. Taft liked to think that his whips gave off the strongest odor of leather, but he knew he was also smelling the vests, the hats, and the moccasins that made up a large part of Lloyd's stock. The cedar odor came from the jewelry boxes, the hope chests, the knick-knack shelves, the knick-knacks, and the plaques which were on display on the wall right beside the front entrance. Lloyd told Taft that the odor of cedar put people in a mood to buy because it made them feel far away from home. Even if they had, say, cedar closets at home, a souvenir stand with a cedar smell would make them feel more comfortable and more likely to buy souvenirs because they'd feel like they were taking a piece of their home back with them.

All of the serious leather goods were displayed along the walls of the trading post. In display cases which formed four narrow aisles down the length of the building, Lloyd offered a variety of Indian jewelry, purses, crafts, stuffed animals, hillbilly geegaws, hats, mountain minerals, carved flutes, drums, bows and arrows, spears, tomahawks, and slingshots. At the end of the central aisle, hanging from wooden pegs, were Taft's whips. From where Taft sat at the cash register, he had a clear view of how people handled his whips. He could also look out the window of the front door and see the cars as they pulled into the trading post parking lot.

Because it was a Wednesday, and a fairly cool April day, Taft didn't expect much business. Too early in the season for big bunches of tourists. But Lloyd was proud that he was one of the few souvenir stand operators who stayed open all year round. What kept them in groceries, though, was Jeanette's job as a school teacher. Lucky for Lloyd that Jeanette had that good insurance coverage with her job. Taft tried to calculate what Lloyd's hospital bill would be with two weeks in intensive care. At least he was out of critical condition.

Without much trouble, Taft thought he could climb into one of the cane bottom rocking chairs, prop his feet up on one of the nail kegs that Lloyd sold as umbrella stands, and doze off. For that matter, Taft admitted, he could just rest his head on the counter and pass out. Then he pictured himself as a bunch of tourists would see him, draped over the counter, dead to the world. That would be worse than some stranger catching him wrestling with the grizzly bear. Besides, on slow days, Taft could listen to the radio and braid another whip for the trading post.

When Taft had first started working at the trading post, he was surprised when Lloyd instructed him to keep the radio on, especially when customers were in the store. Taft was further surprised when the station that Lloyd usually listened to was the same gospel station that Cora cooked and cleaned to at home. Lloyd had never struck Taft as somebody who would appreciate gospel music. Then Lloyd had explained that he wanted the radio to be on during business hours because he believed that a quiet store made the customers nervous. He didn't want the tourists leaving before they'd had time to talk themselves out of not buying anything. Furthermore, according to Lloyd, if gospel music was playing, then customers would think twice about trying to steal or complaining about the prices. Taft understood Lloyd's reasoning, but he wasn't sure if he approved of it.

Around eleven o'clock, as Taft was approaching the end braid of an eight-foot whip and George Beverly Shea was singing "Stand By Me" on the Gospel Ship Jubilee radio program, a Volvo station wagon grumbled across the trading post parking lot and nosed right up to one of the hillbilly dolls sitting in a rocking chair by the front steps.

From his forty years working on lumber hacks and from his two years working at the trading post, Taft had learned to read people's moods by the way they parked. And this fellow in the Volvo was about as nervous a person as Taft had ever seen. Not that long ago, on a slow day at the trading post when Lloyd, Jeanette, and Cora were all sitting around, Jeanette, from the ridge of her education, had told them that people who parked up close to the building or to other cars were anxious about something and wanted to escape to the safety of the womb.

Taft nodded. He'd had days when he wished he had his mama to tell his troubles to. And he'd spent more than one night curled up against Cora when he was afraid to surrender to sleep. Happy people, he admitted, did park right in the middle of the landscape then grin as they crawled out of their cars like they'd brought over your supper. But Taft had always figured that people in bad moods parked close to porches, walls, and other cars just to irritate everybody else.

The man driving the Volvo, though, didn't have anybody else in the parking lot to irritate—unless maybe his wife because she'd have to walk around the back of the car to get to the trading post door. The rear doors of the station wagon bounced open. First to get out was a boy about ten years old; then a second boy, about seven, climbed out, followed closely by a girl about five. They didn't run to the bear the way most children did. Instead, they clumped around the back passenger door and inspected the front of the store, the parking lot, and the concrete animals in front of the trading post. Taft had seen coal miners carried up from a cave-in with fewer reservations about the day than those three children slumped under.

The father eased himself out of the car, braced his hands against the top of the door jamb, then arched his back six or seven times, drooping his head down below his elbows. Meanwhile, the mother studied the factory-made quilts hanging on the line while she rested one arm on the top of the Volvo and draped her other arm over her door. All five of them seemed slightly melted, as if they'd stood all day in front of an open furnace. They were the most unhappy tourists Taft had ever seen in his life.

The Cherokee Trading Post was not the most soothing place to stretch your legs. Taft liked the log walls well enough, but somehow, Lloyd managed to display his goods with a strong element of flutter. It was like being in a chicken house during an electrical storm. Adding to the agitation of the merchandise were those four long glass cases. The longer Taft worked at the trading post, the more those glass cases made him think of caskets. Like that grizzly bear—the glass cases didn't belong in a log cabin even if the whole purpose of the cabin was to tempt the tourists.

But Taft owed Lloyd. That was all Taft wanted to admit. Neither he nor Lloyd could have predicted that the cherry tree would be springy enough to bounce that tree limb back against Lloyd's ladder.

When the man finished stretching his back and herded his children toward the entrance to the trading post, Taft coiled his nearly-braided whip and stored it on the wooden shelf below the cash register. The mother had to run to catch up with her family. Not one of the children or their father glanced back to see if she was with them. Taft watched them for a few seconds longer then turned up the volume on the Gospel Ship Jubilee. An old Carter Family song was playing: "Keep on the Sunny Side." Taft wondered where they could dig up such old records. He'd listened to that song when he was a boy. But he knew he'd never been a boy like either of the two coming through the trading post door.

Both of them were dressed like South American explorers: tan shirts with half a dozen pockets spread across the front, each pocket decorated with some kind of wild animal patch; dark brown corduroy pants held up with bright blue nylon belts. Each boy clomped into the trading post in the kind of boot that nobody in Goshen Hollow ever thought about wearing—thick toothy Vibram soles, red fuzzy shoe strings, and brass lace hooks rather than holes.

Over the years, Taft had seen a few hundred backpackers—although as a rule they stopped at places like the trading post just to mock the stock—but he never could picture how they fit into the woods. He couldn't imagine where they'd look at home in the clothes they wore. Their flannel shirts, their bandanas, their shorts, their wool socks—no matter how grimy they got, they always looked more in uniform than the rangers.

Subdued children always made Taft nervous. Souvenir stores usually brought such children right to the edge of their parents' control because about ninety-eight percent of the time, the parents couldn't bring themselves to give the children what they really wanted. Either the kids wanted something that was too expensive or too dangerous or the parents already had such a stiff notion of what constituted the proper souvenir that the children had to take what was offered them or they wouldn't get any kind of toy.

Like most of the people who lived in Goshen Hollow, Taft spent a great deal of his time speculating about people. In his experience, Volvo parents tended to be more understanding than parents who drove Fords and Chevrolets. But Taft had never seen any tourists as strained as the people who had just stepped inside the trading post. The children didn't have much more vitality than the cement squirrels out beside the parking lot. Their mother and father approached Taft with the weightless motion he usually attributed to people with sore gums.

"Come on in and spread out." Taft leaned both elbows on the counter beside the cash register. "You got the whole store to yourself."

Clumped together, almost in perfect step, the family moved toward Taft. "Are we far from Atlanta?" The father glanced at Taft then let his eyes sweep the contents of the trading post.

Taft rotated his body so he could lean on his right elbow and rub his cheek with his left hand. "Let me see. You go on down this road till you get off the mountain. That's thirty miles. Then after thirty more miles, you'll come to Interstate 77. Get on it and head south to Charlotte, about fifty-five miles, where you'll want to pick up Interstate 85 and head south toward Atlanta. Course, you have to drive through all of South Carolina, so you can count on about eight hours from here." From the slight shriveling that tightened the man's posture, Taft could tell that he'd hoped they were closer to Atlanta.

"Been on the road long?" Taft knew they weren't from North Carolina because everybody raised in the South these days grew up knowing how far he was from Atlanta even if he never planned on visiting the place.

"We left Duluth three days ago." The man ran his fingers through his dark but thinning hair.

"I guess it must still be winter time that far up on the globe." Taft wondered if he still had that issue of Reader's Digest where he had read the article on Minnesota. These folks looked like they might be a little homesick. But some other kind of sadness had its teeth deep in their livers.

"Right now, I'd be willing to trade a month of sunshine for a week of straight, level roads." For the first time, the man really looked at Taft.

In the man's face, Taft could see fairly new lines of disappointment—not exactly wrinkles yet, but well on their way. And the muscles along his jaw looked newly slack too. What Taft saw in the man's face was something like grief, as if some important emptiness had forced his muscles—all of his muscles—to stretch far beyond their normal limits. But the man's grief wasn't connected to a death in the family or a serious illness because that kind of trouble pulled a person's muscles tight.

While Taft talked to the man, the wife and their children moved closer to the counter. The older of the two boys noticed the collection of rubber shrunken heads hanging from the pole across from the cash register. Most of the kids who found the shrunken heads made a grab for them, usually knocking four or five off in the floor. Every mother whom Taft had watched over the last two years felt obligated to ask her child what he wanted with such a nasty-looking toy. Despite the parental objections, the shrunken heads were one of Lloyd's best-selling toys. Taft felt the same way about the shrunken heads as he did about that grizzly bear outside.

Neither one had any business at the Cherokee Trading Post. Neither one was native to the Appalachian Mountains.

For a few seconds, the ten-year-old caressed the squinched features of the shrunken head, but a whispered piece of advice from the mother caused the boy to bury his hands deeply into the pockets of his pants. As irritated as Taft could get when the store was full of arguing, whining, shouting children, this boy's obedience was far more unsettling than any temper tantrum Taft had witnessed.

"It's all right for them children to look around." Taft didn't normally encourage customers to set their offspring loose, but if he had been a horse, Taft would have sworn he could smell fear coming off this family–every single member.

"No." The mother's voice reminded Taft of a dog-chewed chair leg: splintery and bleached out, with a faint wobble. "If they look around too much, they'll start wanting too much. And I don't have the . . ." She allowed her eyes to climb up to her husband's face as she spoke.

"But you ought to let them have something to remember their vacation by." Taft wasn't so much concerned with making a sale as he was with wanting to see the children act more like children. If the mother or the father took offense at his comment, then he'd be relieved to see them leave. If a person was going to travel, then he owed it to everybody he met to hide whatever sorry moods might be riding along with him.

"Just because we're on the move doesn't mean we're on vacation." The man picked up a cedar salt shaker and slowly turned it in his fingers as if he were screwing a lightbulb into an invisible socket.

"Moving?" Taft tried not to sound like he was prying. But this family with its Volvo station wagon outside didn't look like it was moving.

THE SOLAR-POWERED SOUTHERN BELLE

"Fleeing." Keeping her eyes on the floor, the wife led the children past her husband and deeper into the store.

Seeing that the husband wasn't going to answer his wife, Taft studied the station wagon more closely. Now he saw that the car was too loaded up—on the roof luggage rack and in the rear—for a simple vacation or even an innocent move. People like this hired men to carry their furniture, but people like this also followed that big moving truck to their new home. As far as Taft could tell, these people weren't following anything.

"You got a new house down in Atlanta?" Taft felt uncomfortable asking the man, so he directed the question down the aisle toward the woman.

Before she answered, the woman pried a stone-headed tomahawk from the fingers of her daughter. "I have a sister in Atlanta. She has the new house, and we're going to help her break it in." The woman didn't return the tomahawk to the shelf right away. Staring out across the store at her overloaded Volvo, the woman tapped the palm of her hand with the stone of the tomahawk.

Her husband jammed his hands into his back pockets and arched his back. "I'm going down there to find work. The market for my kind of management skills dried up in Duluth."

The man's casual tone was brittle, like a cheap veneer. From it, Taft could guess that there was no moving van leading these people to Atlanta. All they had was out there in their car. Depending on the kind of luck this man had in Atlanta, he and his family might be facing even harder times. And all of them were making this move fully aware of what they had lost—what they might continue to lose. They were all scared.

Taft had to look down at the floor where he slid his shoe back and forth as if trying to erase his desire to feel sorry for these people. He could tell they weren't used to people feeling sorry for them. They weren't used to feeling sorry for themselves. If they had grown up in Goshen Hollow, they wouldn't have any problems with feeling poor or feeling sorry for themselves. Many mornings when Taft had to crawl out of bed with the flu and drive the thirty-three miles to work outside in the lumber yard, he'd felt sorry for himself. At the same time, he was proud of what he was doing, but only a fool would think he had nothing to feel sorry about. The people Taft really felt sorry for were the folks who thought they'd never get chewed on and scratched up by the grizzly bear of misfortune.

Taft felt related to this family once he realized he could feel sorry for them. What irritated him, though, was how dazed they acted, like they'd been sitting around their kerosene heater and it exploded on them.

"You've got a nice set up for yourself here." The man fingered a rawhide vest.

"There's always a steady demand for junk." Taft tried to keep the vague anger he felt under control. "But this place ain't mine." He picked up the whip he'd been working on and came out from behind the counter. "The feller who owns it fell off a ladder a couple weeks ago and is in the hospital with a hundred and sixty stitches in his side."

"He must have fallen an awfully long way." The man took the whip that Taft held out to him.

"Not more than twelve feet. He was outside, right beside this building. I was helping him trim off a limb that was rubbing some of the shingles off the roof." Taft noticed that the man's wife had stood up and was walking toward him and her husband. She had her eyes on the whip which the man had uncoiled and was wiggling on the floor. "We had a rope tied around the limb, and I was supposed to keep that limb from bumping against the side of the trading post. When Lloyd, the feller who owns this place, sawed through the limb, I pulled like I was supposed to, and like we'd planned, the limb swung away from the wall, but it did swing right up against this wild cherry tree."

Taft glanced across the store, wondering where the two boys were, hoping they'd found the whips on their own. Sure enough, both boys stood at the back wall, running their fingers over the leather braids. "If I'd had any sense, I'd have just let go of the rope and let that limb break on through the cherry. But I stood there, holding the rope, watching the cherry tree bend way over with the weight of that cut limb, and then the cherry sprung back. It threw that big old limb right up against Lloyd's ladder. That's what knocked him off. He fell straight down, still standing up, and landed still standing up. The ground was so soft that he wouldn't have hurt himself one bit. Except when the limb hit the ladder, it bashed a big dent in the aluminum, and one of the rungs stuck out–had a piece of ragged metal jutting out from it. From what we could figure, Lloyd must have caught on that rung as he went down, opening up his side from his hip up past his rib cage."

What Taft didn't feel like telling them was how part of Lloyd's lung peeked out of the gash, how he couldn't breathe until Taft had tied him shut with seven or eight strips of rawhide. Taft could tell that this family wouldn't appreciate any more details from someone else's life–not at the moment. He had told them Lloyd's story partly to make himself feel better and partly to introduce them to his whips. The two boys had brought up two six-foot whips. The mother, at some point, had gone back to them and selected an eight-foot whip for herself and a three-foot whip for her daughter.

"You folks have took a beating." Taft watched the family running the leather over their palms and through their fingers.

After two years of making whips, Taft realized that they made people feel connected to power. Not exactly like a gun or a car made a man feel powerful, but in a more personal way—a more personal connection to a more personal power. Although Taft popped every whip he made, he'd never fully identified how he felt each time he saw the length of leather curving through the air. What you flicked with a whip was always something inside.

The man was now slowly popping his wrist, sending a series of lazy waves down the tapered suppleness of his whip. "I tell you—I feel like I've been covering my butt with my heart for the last three years."

"Nobody in Atlanta's going to be happy to see you in that condition." Taft went to the wall and picked out a whip for himself. "I'll give you them whips—if you show me you're ready to start beating back. Whips ain't much good to folks who walk on all fours."

The mother swished her whip back and forth across the floor, but when she looked up at Taft, after glancing at her children and her husband, her eyebrows were still slightly warped with apprehension. "What kind of proof do you want?"

As soon as Taft had pointed out the window across the parking lot and said, "That bear that don't belong," the three children and their parents had rushed out the door. Taft planned to join them, but first, they needed a few minutes alone. And Taft was enjoying the way the children skipped around, popping the bear's legs and crotch while their parents moved with a more sliding sort of grace, aiming for the bear's cracked snarl and cloudy glass eyes. Besides, Taft figured he had all summer to come to terms, his own terms, with that bear.

Preserving the Integrity of the Goshen Valley Dead

Romulus Anderson visited the town of Blowing Rock twice a year at the most. This was the first time in all his life that he'd come here with a reason. Although he'd been making these infrequent visits for nearly forty years, he never got used to the crowds, so he stayed in a constant waver between being amused by all the foreign-looking tourists and being awed by their wealth and easy confidence with all the other strangers on the street. As far back as Romulus could remember, Blowing Rock had always attracted the people with the money and newest cars. It was a town made primarily for visitors and vacationers with its cool nights in the summer and its nearby ski slopes in the winter. And of course, the town had its mountain scenery.

In all of his visits to Blowing Rock, Romulus had never bought anything but an ice cream cone. If he'd had the money and the need, he could have bought real estate, souvenirs, or antiques. If he'd had the money and didn't live but thirty miles down the road, he could have stayed in one of the fifteen or sixteen motels scattered around the town and eaten food he'd never heard of in a few of the twenty-four restaurants doing business in and around Blowing Rock.

But whenever Romulus came to Blowing Rock, he always carried in his mind the conviction that he had absolutely no business in such a town. Until today.

In the past, he and his neighbor, Hugh Garnes, came up when they found themselves vaguely uneasy and restless because many of the people who lived in Wilkes County wanted to keep an eye on what Blowing Rock was doing. Transient as the population of Blowing Rock might seem, more and more people were buying land around the mountain town and building houses on slopes that a bear couldn't climb. Those houses kept inching closer to the Wilkes County line. Already, people with accents that Romulus had never heard–not even on television–were driving on the gravel road down below his house, usually looking for access to the Kerr-Scott Reservoir.

As a rule, Romulus liked people, even when they had accents. True, he had grown up in one of the hollers which radiated up from the valley cut by the Yadkin River–back before it was dammed up and became the Kerr-Scott Reservoir, but being raised in an isolated holler hadn't stunted his sociability. His wife Telitha had grown up just one ridge over from Romulus's family, but she was afraid of strangers. All she needed was Romulus, a grandchild or two, and five or six dogs, and she was happy to stay at home.

Despite how much he liked to talk to his neighbors and people who stopped in the road when they saw him working in his field or hunched over his fishing pole, brooding over the large motionless lake below the road, Romulus didn't trust anybody who was just passing through. Since the state had come along and put gravel on the road that ran below his house, he'd been waiting for the trouble to start. And after twelve years, it had.

"Rom. Look there." Hugh pointed toward the window of an antique store, his elbow bumping Romulus in the stomach.

"Just like Jettie said." Romulus locked his thumb and index finger over his eyebrows to stare in the window. He had to wait for a man and a woman to finish their inspection of the window before he could take the closer look he needed.

Noticing the two farmers in their rather frazzled polyester pants and shirts that didn't want to stay tucked in around their bony hips, the man and woman took each other's hand and slid cautiously back into the sidewalk's main flow of traffic.

The window contained three Tiffany lamps, several shawls, a small writing desk, a three-shelf bookcase, two white marble angel statues—and between the two angels stood an old tombstone weathered down to a graininess that made it look like a gray saltlick instead of very old granite with the name Clifford Anderson carved in an arc along the top. Clifford Anderson was Romulus's great grandfather. And the last time Romulus had looked, about two months ago, that tombstone had been in the family cemetery up on the top of Piney Ridge.

Yesterday, he and Telitha had been in their back yard making their gourd birds. Since they didn't have their children to feed anymore, except maybe on their Sunday visits, Romulus and Telitha didn't have to plant as big a vegetable garden as they once did. But they didn't like the idea of giving up their cultivated land to the woods, so they had begun planting gourds. They had been surprised to find that Lloyd Redwine was willing to sell their gourds at his Cherokee Trading Post. Especially when they had more time in the fall, Romulus sorted through gourds to see which ones made him think of birds and the ones he wasn't inspired by Telitha painted or varnished and turned into vases, bird houses, water dippers, towel holders, and door wreaths.

As he was adding the final coat of varnish to what was going to be an egret, Jettie Francum had driven up and parked almost on top of Romulus's foot. Even before she cut off her engine, Romulus could see that she was carrying news about to make her face snap like a rubber band. Her mouth and cheeks were pulled so tight they looked as if they were attached to a tourniquet.

Jettie was talking as soon as she hit the ground. "Rom, Telitha, you got to get up to Blowing Rock." She stood beside one of the spare metal lawn chairs to emphasize that she was too upset to sit down.

Not long after his fifty-first birthday, Romulus had noticed that it took him a lot longer to get alarmed than it used to. One of his boys had told him that he wasn't getting wiser, his reflexes were just getting slower. Romulus didn't care what the reason was, all he valued was the relief he felt when he discovered that he didn't have to jump every time a Jettie Francum looked at him with her eyes bulging from bad news. From the way Telitha settled back in her chair and studied Jettie, Romulus could tell that her capacity for alarm had also diminished to the size of curiosity.

"What's in Blowing Rock?" Romulus leaned forward in his chair but kept brushing the varnish on his egret.

"From what my daughter-in-law says, it might be one of your family tombstones." Jettie tilted slightly forward and tapped her knuckles on the top of the chair beside her. "She saw a tombstone in an antique store up there with the name of Clifford Anderson. That was your great grandfather, wasn't it?"

Everyone around Goshen Holler knew Clifford Anderson. He was the man most responsible for bringing moonshine into the county. Back around the 1880's, he had been the richest man ever to come from Wilkes who hadn't gone into politics or chicken farming. He'd owned three grocery stores, seven hundred acres of land, and five stills. What really kept Clifford Anderson's name alive around Wilkes, though, was the quality of his liquor. Of course, all the men who had known Clifford were long since dead, but Romulus had met a few when he was a boy. All of those men, despite how vividly they might recall the names of their own grandfathers, children, and wives, remembered even more profoundly the taste of Clifford Anderson's whiskey.

No doubt, what really helped preserve Clifford's name in the collective memory of Goshen Holler was the fact that the whiskey was still available—in limited quantities.

Granted, the small five-gallon still was in Romulus's basement, but he had never had anything to do with making it. His father, a devout Baptist, had refused to teach Romulus the recipe. And he had, just a few minutes before he died from a herd of tumors in his lungs and brain, made his father, Vernon, swear never to teach Romulus the family secret.

Before going into the antique store, Romulus let his eyes roam around as much of the shop's contents as he could. Many years ago, he'd worked up the courage to go inside one of these places. He'd seen antiques before, plenty of his and Telitha's family and neighbors had antiques.

But Romulus had never been surrounded by antiques up until that day he stepped into the shop with the gramaphone in the window. Although he'd been scared down to the roots of his teeth during his one visit to an operating room, Romulus thought he had more business in one of them than he did in that antique shop. He didn't even have to look at the price tags to know he didn't have any business in such a place. His reflection in a softly glowing hall tree's mirror showed him how out of place he was with his hair combed all wrong then mussed by the drive up the mountain. On a shelf right beside the hall tree, a blue vase emphasized the boniness of Romulus's jaw, and a small tapestry revealed to Romulus how much his best shirt had faded.

While Romulus was trying to control his impulse to bolt out of the place, a thin young man almost a foot taller than Romulus had flowed out from between two grandfather clocks and asked if he could be of help. The young man himself looked like an antique with his wire-rimmed glasses and his satin vest. Romulus didn't think he could even afford a conversation with the man, but he didn't want to seem stupid as well as poor, so he had asked about the price of the gramophone in the window. For what it cost, Romulus could feed his chickens for seven months. He'd told the young man that he'd have to wait until he had a sale. When the man didn't crack a smile, Romulus backed out the door without another word.

Now here he was, years later about to accuse another antique dealer of stealing his great grandfather's tombstone. "You ever had to ask a man how he come by your great granddaddy's tombstone?" Romulus shuffled back to stand beside Hugh.

"It stumps me." Hugh rubbed his cheek with the middle knuckle of his index finger. "He might not know it's stolen. Sometimes, these dealers use people they call pickers who go and pick out the antiques for them."

"So this feller might not know he's got a illegal tombstone on display." Romulus felt a little better about having to go into the shop–if he could hope to have a reasonable talk with the man who ran it.

"As long as you got the death certificate, I don't see how he'd have much room to argue with you." Hugh looked up and down the crowded street. "It might come down to him or us calling in the law."

"Will it bother you, making a scene like that?" Romulus felt his heart speeding up. He had no special respect for the police, but he dreaded having all these polished tourists looking at him. "You can go back and wait in the car if you want to."

"Don't bother me none." Hugh crossed his arms and tilted his chin toward the window. "I figure that old boy in there's got more explaining to do than us. Anybody walking by this winder is going to see that tombstone ain't where it belongs."

"Does make you wonder about the man's judgment, don't it?" Romulus pushed open the door to the shop.

Like most of the shops in Blowing Rock, the antique store was scented with a blend of wood polish, cinnamon, and eucalyptus. Once, Telitha had bought a few sprigs of eucalyptus. The smell was fresh, and she had told Romulus that she liked the idea it had come from Australia by way of Peru—or so she'd been told by the woman at the flower store. Dried flowers of any kind made Romulus a little nervous. They reminded him of the tourists in Blowing Rock. The smell of dried eucalyptus made Romulus think of men in suits and top hats, what he suspected the tourists wore when they got out of their bright shirts and shorts.

What Romulus most disliked about antique stores was how crowded they felt. Little fragile unstable shelves stocked with crystal animals and goblets everywhere he turned. The floor was studded with wooden cats, woven baskets, brass fireplace tools, mahogany umbrella stands, glossy steamer trunks.

Romulus wondered if maybe he should be trying to get his great grandfather's stone back from this place. He imagined some sleek, wealthy woman with small feet and narrow hips weaving smoothly through all these antiques just to claim Clifford Anderson's tombstone so she could carry it back to some mansion in Charlotte or Raleigh or even Atlanta. Who was to say having the tombstone sitting on somebody's marble fireplace mantle might not do more honor to his great grandfather's memory than keeping it stuck in the ground out in some lonely, usually grown up little cemetery?

"You think maybe this feller knows something about tombstones that we don't?" Romulus craned his neck, wondering why people who ran fancy shops always knew who they didn't have to hurry up to wait on.

"All that matters is what we know." Hugh put his fingers in his back pockets and glanced around for a place to lean against. "Uncomfortable little place, ain't it?"

"You afraid if you don't put your hands in your pockets they'll wind up some place they don't belong?" Romulus took five or six more steps toward the back of the shop. He heard his voice going louder as he spoke. Impatience was a problem for him only when he dreaded what he waited for.

"I've just always had a special reverence for things I can't afford." Hugh stayed by the front door.

Romulus understood what Hugh meant. The longer he spent surrounded by these antiques–some of them could have been from flying saucers for all he knew about them– the more cramped he felt. He and Hugh knew they didn't usually have any business in a place like this. But today, for the next few minutes, they did. And Romulus wanted to get it over with. He figured nobody was going to mistake him for a tourist in search of the right set of alabaster bookends to decorate his summer home on the outskirts of town, so Romulus decided to go ahead and act like these people expected him to act.

"Hey! Anybody running this place?" Although Romulus didn't cup his hands around his mouth the way he did when was calling their five hogs out of the woods, he did tilt back slightly and let his voice bounce up from his stomach and off the roof of his mouth.

From a narrow door in the back corner of the shop a woman appeared, her head dipped down, a chocolate covered doughnut in her mouth, her other hand cupped below her chin to catch crumbs. She had the smoothest, whitest hair Romulus had ever seen. With her head still bowed, she looked up at him with light blue eyes over the tops of tortoise shell glasses. Romulus couldn't tell if she was a very old looking young woman or a very young looking old woman.

Expecting to deal with a man, Romulus had been preparing himself all morning to just dig in with his hind legs and not be pushed around. He planned to leave with Clifford Anderson's tombstone even if he had to spend the night in jail for assault—not that he really expected one of these antique store dealers to come to blows with him. They had their inventory to worry about. But Romulus knew he couldn't get too loud against a woman. The only woman he felt comfortable arguing with was Telitha. It was a form of intimacy only a husband and wife should share, as far as Romulus was concerned.

"I'm sorry I didn't come out sooner." The woman lifted her head from her doughnut and smiled. She had chocolate in the corners of her mouth.

"No, no. That's all right. I'm sorry I raised my voice like I did. Nothing worse than some loudmouth stomping in on your breakfast." Romulus bobbed his head a couple of times and fanned his hands out to the side like the fins of a sleepy fish, trying to appease and soothe the woman at the same time. "You ought to sic the dogs on me." He flicked his thumb in the direction of two full-sized ceramic grayhounds.

"I'd get more response if I tried to sic my doughnut on you." The woman smiled.

Despite the chocolate stains, Romulus saw that she had the straightest teeth he'd ever witnessed. Either they were her own, or she wore dentures like an artist, like she had practiced for years before coming out in public. When Romulus caught a glimpse of her gums, he was inclined to believe the teeth were part of the woman. The skin wasn't too pink or purple. All Romulus wanted to see was some sign that the woman might be dishonest. It was much easier for him to be stubborn with people he didn't trust.

"Our business won't take long and then you can get back to your breakfast." Romulus glanced over his shoulder at Hugh, wishing now that his neighbor had stayed in the car. Two men in the shop was too much pressure. Too much like a rough-neck threat.

"Don't be in any hurry." The woman licked her finger and fixed her eyes more firmly on Romulus's face.

He shifted his weight from one foot to the other by cocking his hip to one side then hooked his thumbs in his back pockets. "No. I'm not meaning to siphon off your time. I'm here with a concern. And it makes me uncomfortable to . . ."

"Rom! Just ask about the tombstone." Hugh didn't budge from his spot in front of the door, but he'd fanned out his elbows and puffed out his stomach, bobbing slightly as he spoke.

The woman, lowering the doughnut to her side, but keeping it away from the gray slacks she wore, looked over Romulus's head and frowned in Hugh's direction, but Romulus could tell that she was frowning more for herself than for Hugh.

"You mean that tombstone in the window?" She turned her eyes back to Romulus.

"Clifford Anderson was my great granddaddy." Romulus pulled from his back pocket a folded death certificate and handed it to the woman. "That tombstone was in my family cemetery not two months ago, and I'm mighty confused about it being in your winder now."

"Lord, I knew those two were trouble as soon as they carried that stone into the shop." The woman read the certificate, shaking her head. "I got my own picker, and he's never brought me a tombstone." She continued to stare at the paper. "So now I'm doing business with grave robbers."

"It's not that bad." Romulus thought about patting her shoulder, but this was a Blowing Rock antique store—not the Goshen Baptist Church. She had to know that he'd come to get the stone, not just talk about it.

"I am so sorry." The woman handed Romulus the death certificate and slumped, her spine taking on the curve of an ancient floor lamp beside her. "This is the worst I've ever felt since I started selling antiques."

"Take another bite of doughnut." Romulus clasped his hands and rolled his knuckles toward her pastry. "It'll make you feel better."

The woman did take another bite. "All my instincts told me those two boys were lying. They said it'd come from a cemetery that had been bought by a company that was requiring all the graves—old and new—to put in those brass plaques. The kind that're flush to the ground so it's easier to mow."

"I know the kind of arrangement you're talking about." Romulus was beginning to feel worse than if he'd been in a yelling match. "But a man with a good weed eater don't have any special problems with the old style tombstones."

"Well, what do you want to do about the theft?" The woman took a deep breath and made a weak attempt to square her shoulders.

"If you'll agree to it, I'd like to take the stone back home with me." Romulus bowed slightly toward the woman and cocked his left ear in her direction, prompting her for an answer.

"Of course, I'll agree to return the stone. It's yours." The woman stepped closer to Romulus and leaned within a few inches of his face. "But don't you want to see if the police'll investigate the two boys? I can give you a description of them. They drive a white van. A Ford Econoline. One of the big ones, you know. They parked it right in front of my shop when they unloaded the stone."

"The police wouldn't care much about us getting robbed." Hugh walked over to the front window.

Romulus edged to one side and let the woman walk by him on her way to the window. "I'll just have to keep a better eye on the place."

Stopping in mid-stride, the woman jerked around to face Romulus. "Let me tell you, they talked like they planned on bringing in a few more tombstones."

"How much did you pay for Clifford's stone?" Hugh peered over the bookcase which made up part of the window display's background but didn't attempt to touch any of the antiques around the tombstone.

"They let me have it for fifty dollars." The woman focused her attention on sliding the bookcase to the side then shifting the two angels away from the stone.

"How many tombstones you got in your cemetery, Rom?" Hugh puckered his eyebrows.

"Seventy? A hundred?" Romulus shrugged. "A bunch."

"I hope there's a comfortable place for you to sleep up there on that hill because that's what you're going to have to do." Hugh stooped over and took hold of the stone. "Why'd a man as rich as Clifford Anderson not get a bigger stone?"

Romulus got on the other side of the stone and helped Hugh lift it out of the window. Small as it was, it'd still be enough of a job for them to carry it back to the car. "A moonshiner spends a big part of his life not calling attention to himself. From what Grandpaw Vernon used to tell, Clifford let all his family know that death was not the occasion to forsake his modesty."

Both men had worked up a thick sweat by the time they got the tombstone back to Romulus's car, a 1975 Plymouth Duster. After propping the tombstone against the car's back bumper, Romulus squatted down, preparing to untwist the coat hanger that held his trunk lid shut.

"You sure you want to put your great granddaddy's stone in the trunk like it was a flat tire?" Hugh rubbed his hands together slowly, his calluses scraped across each other, sounding like a small dog coughing.

With a slight shift of his weight from one foot to the other, Romulus turned his attention from the coat hanger to the tombstone. "I guess if a bunch of strangers think enough of it to display it in a Blowing Rock store winder, I ought to pay it enough respect to let it ride in the backseat."

Once he and Hugh got the stone steady in the back, Romulus remembered he was supposed to be carrying another passenger back to Goshen Holler—his grandfather, Vernon Anderson. The Grandin Rest Home where Vernon lived three weeks out of every month was right on the highway that connected Goshen Valley to Blowing Rock. As Romulus was leaving this morning, Telitha had told him to go ahead and bring Vernon back with him since he was going to be up that way.

Vernon had turned ninety last month. He'd spent the last ten years in that rest home. Up until he was eighty, he'd lived with Romulus and Telitha. But he hadn't been happy, hadn't felt at home since they'd moved from the old homestead to the new house up on the ridge. The old house–the one where Vernon had been born, where Romulus's father, Benjamin, had been born, where Romulus was born, where his own children had been born–had been torn down by the government because it would have been under water after the new dam was built. Of course, Romulus had been paid well for the old house and the three hundred acres that went under with it.

He and Telitha had built a fine house that looked down on their little part of the lake. For the first time in his life, Romulus had a basement, not just a crawl hole for the spiders, but a full-sized basement with its own set of windows that faced the lake. They'd put in a bathroom and a little kitchen down there just so Vernon would feel like he still had some independence. But all he'd do was sleep in his new place.

From the first day they'd moved him in, all Vernon had done was complain and talk about the old place and the people who were dead or about dead. On days when he was especially irritated, Vernon insisted that the government ought to go ahead and just drown the whole blamed valley. Just pour a few more feet of concrete on top of the dam and let the water back up over every housetop in the county.

Then the old man got to wandering off. Sometimes, Romulus could find him down by the lake, staring out toward where the old house used to stand. Other times, Romulus had to tromp up the dirt road and climb the hill to the family cemetery. The worst times, though, were those when Vernon ambled off into the woods. At first, Romulus thought perhaps his grandfather had lost his mind, but then he discovered that the spots where he found Vernon were places where he'd once built his moonshine stills.

Although Vernon carried around in his brain the recipe for the moonshine which had made his father, Clifford Anderson, famous, he had respected his dying son's request that he not pass the knowledge on to Romulus.

Hoping to put some use back into his grandfather's life, Romulus asked Vernon if he'd feel better about living in the new house if he could have a small still in his basement. One of Romulus's sons who'd just come home on furlow from the navy had always been clever with his hands. Following Vernon's instructions and making a few improvements on his own, Romulus's son worked for a week to produce the cleanest looking illegal distillery anybody in Wilkes County had ever seen.

As far as the law was concerned, Romulus admitted that thanks to his son's design, the still in the basement was risk free. Small as it was, the boiler–made from a modified pressure cooker–could sit on the electric stove in Vernon's little kitchen. There would be no smoke in the woods to give the state police a curiousity to go see what was causing it. Another drawback to the big old-timey stills was that they had to be set up next to a stream so the moonshiners would have enough running water to cool the coil, the worm, and cause the distilled whiskey to condense. Vernon's little still had its own built-on refrigerator unit around the worm.

Because the still was limited to five-gallon runs, Romulus didn't feel too guilty about going against his father's deathbed wish for the family to be free from its moonshining tradition. At that time, in a county like Wilkes, five gallons didn't qualify as serious distilling. Besides, Romulus and Telitha had agreed that Vernon couldn't run his still on a regular basis. They figured one five-gallon run a month was all he needed to keep feeling useful. And they gave the moonshine away, only to people who were the same age as Vernon or older.

From the very start, the still caused trouble. As long as Vernon was waiting for the mash to ferment, as long as he had the still fired up, he behaved himself. But when he fully realized that Romulus and Telitha meant to limit his runs to five gallons a month, he got harder to manage. Before they let him have the still–to the best of Romulus's knowledge–Vernon had kept his promise to Benjamin. He'd gone for nearly eighteen years without making moonshine or even talking about it to Romulus.

Then to be exposed once again to the pleasure of creating the drink that had made his father famous and rich for a while pulled Vernon off of his promise like some big snake pulling an eagle off of its nest. At first, all Romulus and Telitha had to do to control Vernon was just to let him know they were keeping an eye on him. Of course, they had to stop visiting other relatives, and if they needed to be gone longer than three or four hours for shopping or going to the doctor, one of them either had to stay at home or they had to get somebody to come and watch Vernon. They had learned that he had started fermenting mash in the woods and sneaking it into his basement. All he needed was two or three hours to distill it.

Neither Romulus nor Telitha felt too imposed upon having to monitor Vernon's basement, and they might never have put him in the rest home except Telitha began having more and more trouble with her arthritis and her phlebitis. Romulus had to take her occasionally all the way to Winston-Salem–sixty miles away–for treatment. It never failed but when he and Telitha walked back in the house, they could count on being greeted by the curvy smell of freshly distilled whiskey.

When it seemed like they might be getting Telitha straighted out, Romulus discovered a growth on his chest. He waited a few months, hoping the knot would go away. Instead it got bigger until Telitha saw it through his t-shirt. Facing an operation, at least two weeks in the hospital, and another few weeks in his bed, Romulus agreed with Telitha that they could no longer control Vernon. Rather than cooperating, the old man shamelessly took full advantage of all the hours Romulus and Telitha were spending at the doctors'.

As if the small still wasn't enough, Vernon had begun acting the way he used to, back before 1965 when he made his promise to his dying son, when he was operating the larger more illegal stills off in the woods. More than once, Romulus had seen the old man carrying lumber off into the woods. If he was indeed building a big still and if he did get caught, and if the still was on Romulus's property, then they'd all be in trouble. All he and Telitha could do to protect themselves was to put Vernon in the Grandin Rest Home.

Vernon had been the first Anderson from Goshen Holler to be put in a rest home. Romulus suffered more from that shame than he had recuperating from his cancer surgery. While he still struggled with the shame, he also had to bottle up the regret he felt when he saw how Vernon became an old man so certainly after spending a few months with other old people.

Out of her own shame, Telitha had been the one to suggest bringing him home once a month and letting him cook a run of whiskey. Several ailing elderly citizens of Goshen Holler had been phoning and visiting on a regular basis, complaining to Telitha and Romulus about how much they missed the glow of Vernon's moonshine. To soothe his conscience, Romulus drove Vernon around the county after he'd distilled his five gallons and helped him deliver the pint jars to the people who needed it most that month.

After ten years of coming to pick up his grandfather at the rest home, Romulus still felt his stomach tighten when he pulled into the driveway that curved up the hill toward the low brick building which could easily be mistaken for an old motel since that was what it used to be.

"You going to move here when you get too old and ugly to live with your family?" Hugh had come with Romulus to the rest home often enough to develop his own dread of the place.

"If it's good enough for my grandfather, I guess it'll be good enough for me." Romulus parked in front of a box shrub. He wanted to get a deep whiff of one green bush before he went inside the rest home.

"Just try to stay sweet enough and maybe you won't wind up here." Hugh propped his knees up against the dashboard. He'd ride up with Romulus, but long ago, he'd stopped offering to go in with him.

The air in the lobby of the rest home made Romulus feel as if his shirt was too small across his chest and stomach. More than the smell of old folks who didn't get bathed but once a week, what made Romulus's clothes tighten around him was the smell of inactivity. Parked here and there in their wheelchairs or bent stiffly onto a couch or chair, the citizens of the rest home reminded Romulus of the driftwood that piled up in the dead corners of shadowy bays along the lake, deposited there by waves that had been swallowed by the muddy banks.

Behind a counter that was too long for a rest home lobby but about right for a motel lobby, a woman in a nurse's uniform recognized Romulus. "You here to visit or you planning to take Vernon home for his visit?" She checked her clipboard. "He's getting his shave right now, back in the social hall."

Knowing from his ten years of visits that this woman, Kayette, like all the other reception nurses who had sat at the counter before her, didn't like to lose contact with the old people stored in the lobby, Romulus gave her a doorknob wave on his way past. "I'll get him packed up. No need for you to bother yourself." Romulus wondered if he'd ever completely digest the guilt he felt about keeping Vernon in this place.

To get to his grandfather's room, Romulus had to walk by the social hall. Back when the rest home had been a motel, it must have advertised its indoor pool. One of the managers at the King Chicken Processing Plant, when he found out that Romulus had put his grandfather in the rest home, had told him that when the place first started taking care of old people, the owners had tried to keep the pool operating because they thought water sports would appeal to their guests.

What they hadn't counted on was the fact that many of their guests had grown up in such a rural area that the concept of a swimming pool struck them as somehow indecent or at least nasty. Many of the old people, raised in isolated hollers or lonely ridges regarded old age as the time they could be left alone with family albums or Bibles. Yes, they were lonely people, but not many of them saw splashing around in a pool as a way to cure what they felt as a result of their families' abandoning them. Eventually, the owners put a cheap parquet floor over the pool, bought a phonograph, and hired a P.E. teacher from the high school to teach the old people folk and social dance. Too many old Baptists in the home put dancing in the same category as getting into a pool with a bunch of people they'd never known well enough to share a bath with, and after three years, the P.E. teacher stopped coming by, leading the owners to invest in a few card tables, one barber chair, and three salon chairs. Even when the barber or the beautician wasn't on duty, the old people gathered around the chairs and discussed their problems.

As Romulus passed the windows that looked into the social hall, he saw that Vernon was in the process of getting his neck shaved. At least twelve other men sat in a semi-circle of folding chairs waiting their turn. After ten years of observing, Romulus had noticed that each year, Vernon's neck got more and more saggy until the barber had to tilt the old man's head back almost to his neck to get the skin taut enough for the razor to do its job. But even with his head arched until his adam's apple looked like it was about pop up into the fluorescent light above the chair, Vernon was talking.

You couldn't exactly call Vernon's conversation lively. After all these years, Romulus wasn't sure if he could even make himself listen to what Vernon had to say. Those three years just before he and Telitha had put Vernon in this place, all he heard from Vernon was lies about his moonshining. Romulus couldn't stand his memory of Vernon standing over his little still down in the basement kitchen and even as the moonshine was dripping out of the condenser, Vernon would deny that he had snuck off in the woods and fermented another batch of mash, when right there behind him on the counter was the little wooden barrel of beer.

Then too, the old man was fond of talking about Romulus's father back before he got saved and spent all of his spare time moonshining and bootlegging. For a little while, Benjamin Anderson was a celebrity because he had helped the movie people who came to Wilkes to film Thunder Road—back in 1955. He'd showed Robert Mitchum how a bootlegger would drive a car. Once he was saved, though, Benjamin had always felt more guilty about that part of his life than any other. Millions of people had seen that movie, he'd told the congregation of the Goshen Baptist Church, and it had made them think moonshining was some kind of admirable work. And he, Benjamin Anderson, had helped with that devil's message. The congregation forgave Benjamin long before he forgave himself. If he ever forgave himself.

One reason Romulus didn't like to hear Vernon talk about Thunder Road was because he knew that his wreck was what caused his father to get converted. Like most of the boys in Wilkes County, Romulus had been driving since he was eleven or twelve. But shortly after the movie people had gone back to Hollywood, Romulus had gotten his driver's license. He and Benjamin were coming back from town along a curvy dirt road, the same road where Robert Mitchum had forced the crook driver off the edge. Without slowing down, Romulus eased the car to the very edge of the road which overlooked the gorge, about two hundred feet straight down. His daddy had told him to because he wanted to see if he could find the wreckage of the car the movie people had rolled down the bank then couldn't get back up.

The front tires had taken a bite on the loose edge and jumped over the side of the gorge. Romulus had been thrown over against his daddy. Both of them broke ribs when the car slammed against a couple of thick oak trees. Benjamin had been hurt more than Romulus because he'd caught his son's weight on one side of his ribs and his own weight on the elbow rest. He'd coughed up blood after they climbed back up the bank and started walking home. Before they got back to the house, Benjamin had passed out twice and started having trouble getting enough air.

Barely two years after the wreck, Romulus's father was not only born again but he had become a preacher himself. Eight years later, he was dead.

Baylus Poteat had taken over the serious moonshining business as soon as he heard that Benjamin Anderson was giving up the family tradition. Baylus had taught his sons the business. Romulus had to admit that many were the days when he was breaking his back shoveling manure in his chicken houses that he wished his father had trusted him with Clifford Anderson's secrets. At times, especially in the summer when the ammonia from the chicken house was enough to blind him as he checked their automatic feeders and waterers, Romulus wished he hadn't sworn to his dying father that he would never let Vernon teach him the Anderson distillery secrets.

Of course, Baylus Poteat didn't have it all that easy either. Romulus knew enough about moonshining to know that it was a rough life. Then in the early seventies, the big moonshine trade dried up. Too much technology. Too much smoke from a still. And all the agents had to do was come tramping down along all the little streams in the county. Baylus and his boys had bought up a lot of land and kept their eye on the growing markets. They'd moved from moonshine to marijuana.

There was an ugly business, Romulus thought. Too rough for him. He delivered a pint of Vernon's brew to Baylus's trailer because his wife used the whiskey to make some of her own medicine. She mixed part of the whiskey with ground up camphor berries and used the paste as a disinfectant which could be taken both internally and externally. She also made her own cough drops by draining the juice out of a jar of maraschino cherries and replacing it with Vernon's moonshine.

But going to Baylus's trailer was like visiting an armed camp. Even before you got to the trailer, you had to survive Baylus's dogs. Most of the people in Goshen Holler believed that Baylus advertised for mean dogs. Anytime somebody's dog gave birth to a puppy that snarled at the children and killed chickens, the advice always came: "Give it to Baylus."

The trailer itself had been double sided with sheet metal. The one concession that Baylus had made to his wife was that he'd had the sheet metal painted pale blue. One of his five sons had suggested they paint it camouflage, but Baylus's wife said she wouldn't live in a house that looked like it came from the army surplus store. Of course, the inside of the trailer looked like an army surplus store. At any time of the day or night, one of Baylus's sons was sitting on the porch of the trailer with a shotgun across his lap and a scoped M-16 leaning against his rocking chair.

If Vernon was grateful to get away from the rest home one week out of each month, he never showed it. Then again, Vernon seldom showed anything. As Romulus watched his grandfather slide out of the barber's chair, gather his strength and balance, then angle toward the door, like a sailboat in a contrary wind, he admitted to himself that except for that little zigzag in his walk, Vernon didn't show much of his age.

As soon as the old man stepped into the hallway, he saw Romulus. He studied his grandson for several seconds, stroking his chin. "Time for my ride? Already?"

"It's a couple days early, Powpaw." Romulus swung the old man's child-size suitcase in front of his knees, signaling to Vernon that they didn't have to go back to his room. It didn't matter much what Romulus put in the old man's suitcase because he had more clothes at home than he did in the rest home. But from what Romulus had learned over the years, the suitcase made the trip home feel more substantial to Vernon.

"Somebody sick?" Vernon leaned into his walk as if gravity was working on him from two directions instead of one.

"Well, you know in Wilkes somebody's always sick." Romulus pushed the door open for Vernon. "But nobody in particular. I was just up this way and thought I'd save myself a trip." Romulus cupped his hand over Vernon's bony shoulder and pointed him toward the car.

"That looks like Hugh Garnes with his elbow hanging out the winder." Vernon stooped down, his neck stiff and parallel to the ground so he could better study Hugh.

Hugh threw his arm in a sloppy wave. "You want to ride up front, Mr. Anderson?" He cracked open his door.

"You dip snuff, Hugh?" Vernon grabbed hold of the door and leaned close to Hugh's face.

"When I can't get nothing else." Hugh glanced at Romulus.

"Do you spit or drip when you got a lip full?" Vernon braced one knee against the side of the car to keep steady.

"I usually have me a little cup or jar to drip into."

"Then I'll be happy to ride in the back." Vernon side-stepped to the back door, used both hands to pull it open, then dropped into the seat. Before closing his door, he leaned forward, bringing his head even with Hugh's. "I won't ride in the back if the people in front are spitting out the window. Worst feeling in the world is somebody else's tobacco juice landing in your face."

They'd gone about two miles down the road before Vernon noticed the tombstone in the backseat beside him. Although Romulus had let himself get too preoccupied about how he was going to guard the family cemetery to pay attention to his grandfather, he did notice that Hugh had shifted around in his seat and was watching the old man closely. As soon as Romulus heard Vernon's "What the lord is this?" he realized that Hugh had been just waiting for the old man to discover the tombstone.

"It's your daddy's tombstone." Romulus adjusted the rear-view mirror so he could look at Vernon's face.

The old man leaned around the stone, rubbed his fingers along its edge, then leaned back in his seat. "Clifford Anderson. Born 1850. Died 1924. My daddy. He was a mighty smart man."

"Never once got caught by the revenuers, did he?" Hugh had grown up, like most of the Wilkes County boys, hearing the legend of Clifford Anderson.

"They never even considered trying to catch him." Vernon looked across Hugh's shoulder, studying the lower peaks of the Brushy Mountains. "That's how smart he was. He was an outlaw they left alone. Any melon head can be an outlaw and get chased for it."

As much as Romulus didn't like to encourage Vernon to wallow around in the family's moonshine past, today he felt like he owed the old man a little indulgence. "Clifford might have come out even more famous if the law had come after him a time or two."

Vernon scooted forward to the edge of his seat. "Daddy wasn't concerned about being famous. What he wanted was to be remembered."

"Well, famous outlaws get remembered." Vernon waved a handful of outstretched fingers in Vernon's face. "Look at Tom Duley. He even got a song wrote about him."

His face puckering way beyond his ninety years worth of wrinkles, Vernon slapped at Hugh's hand. "Don't try to tell me anything about Tom Duley. My daddy sold him moonshine–give it to him the biggest part of the time because he didn't usually have enough money to pay for it. My daddy drove a wagon thirty-some miles down to Statesville on May 1, 1868 to watch them hang Tom Duley. 'Course, he conducted some business before and after the hanging because all the saloons was closed on days the town hosted executions. He was just eighteen but he was already working on being remembered by the county where he lived. People like Tom Duley ain't remembered–they're misremembered."

Taking his eyes off the road much longer than he knew to be safe, Romulus tried to uncover in his grandfather's face

where that word, "misremembered," had come from. He'd
heard the story about Clifford going to Tom Duley's hanging
and he'd heard about Clifford wanting to be remembered. But
now, at the age of ninety, Vernon seemed to be adding something just a little new to his stories.

"Times didn't get rough on moonshiners until 1876 when
President Grant hired Green B. Raum to enforce the whiskey
tax. He was the man who turned people against moonshining.
He got neighbors to spy on neighbors, wives to spy on their
husbands." Vernon leaned back in his seat. "But how many
people in Wilkes County remember Green B. Raum?"

"First time I've heard the name." Hugh shook his head but
couldn't take his eyes off the old man.

"Old Green B. Raum and his bunch brought down some
good men, some good moonshiners: Lewis Redmond, Amos
Owens, Bill Berong."

"But not Clifford Anderson." Romulus felt his foot get
heavy on the accelerator.

"Because them other fellers was in it for the wrong reasons."
Vernon pulled himself further back in the seat so he could rest
his back in the corner and get a better view of his grandson.

"So it's okay to make illegal whiskey as long as you got the
right reasons to do it?" Hugh twisted around even further in
his seat to see Vernon's face.

Ignoring Hugh's stare, Vernon leaned toward Romulus.
"There's some of us who never recognized our whiskey as illegal.
Just the big distilleries trying to tell us what to do. How can
something you make with your own two hands that don't kill
nobody be illegal?"

"All I know is my daddy was ashamed he moonshined."
Romulus looked across his shoulder at his grandfather but
didn't give the old man enough time to catch his eyes.

"Your daddy died too soon." Vernon leaned back and stared at the ceiling of the car. Then in jerky increments, the old man turned his attention back to the tombstone beside him. "Just why are you two boys hauling my daddy's tombstone around?"

"Powpaw, it was stolen." Romulus looked back at Vernon and shook his head.

"Turns out that stone is worth fifty dollars to folks who don't even know Clifford Anderson." Hugh tapped Vernon's knee and nodded. "Think for a minute about how many exposed tombstones you still have left in your family cemetery and multiply that by fifty dollars. . ."

"A hundred and four." Vernon crossed his arms over his chest, his chin bobbed on his left shoulder. "A hundred and five counting Daddy's stone."

"I didn't know you had that many relatives up there." Hugh punched Romulus in the shoulder. "You going to have a big job guarding all them folks."

"We'd had a lot more kin in the ground up there today if the Flood of 1930 hadn't washed away the road so bad that the state had to run their new one all the way on the other side of the river from where it used to be." Vernon rubbed the back of his neck then checked his palm for loose hairs from his haircut. "What was left of the road was too rough for people to drive on."

"And it's just got rougher ever since." Romulus thought about the deep ruts that cut through the trees. Five or six times, the ruts were swallowed by gulleys that cut across the roadbed. Whoever had driven up that steep hill had been mighty determined to make a profit. Romulus couldn't remember the last time he'd tried driving up to the family cemetery. All the dead people he knew were buried in various Baptist cemeteries around the county.

"The last person I saw put in the ground up on Piney Ridge was my Aunt Loretta in 1928. The funeral home still used a horse drawn wagon for a hearse, especially when they had to bury people up in the hills." Vernon shifted in his seat as if some of his haircut had gotten down his shirt. Then he leaned forward to rest his elbows on the seat in front of him. "Mightn't them fellers come back for a few more tombstones?"

"I'd say if they was mean enough to climb up there for fifty dollars they'd be mean enough to come back for six or seven hundred more." Romulus could smell the Club Man aftershave the barber had patted on his grandfather's cheeks and neck. The scent went well with the old man's own odor of dry flesh and confined movement.

"That truck they drive 'sgot to be four-wheel." Hugh tapped the dashboard.

"I guess I will have to spend the nights up there." Romulus wondered how he'd run his chicken business and guard the cemetery. As isolated as the place was, a determined thief wouldn't have to wait until dark to climb up the washed out road to pull up a few more markers. He knew he couldn't interest his sons in taking shifts to watch the tombstones of relatives who'd died long before any of them were born.

"I guess you'll get yourself shot too." Vernon looked straight ahead, his arms hanging between Romulus and Hugh.

"He's right, Rom." Hugh's voice dropped, as if it had tripped over a sudden realization. "Men who'll steal tombstones will likely stoop to anything if they think they can get away with it."

"They're just low is all." Romulus felt suddenly bitter. He'd grown up in Goshen Holler, worked hard, and here he was—threatened by men who couldn't do any better than rob an old cemetery. And his neighbor and grandfather sat there telling him they were too dangerous for him. Without a doubt, Telitha would tell him the same thing. "I guess we could see what the sheriff would do."

"Not much." Hugh laughed. "Him and his boys have trouble protecting the live citizens. I can see you asking him to patrol Piney Ridge."

"There's them that wouldn't be happy with deputies cruising through the holler." Vernon squeezed his hands together, still looking out the windshield. "The person who'll help you, Romulus, is the man who stands to lose more than we do with a bunch of sorry bottom feeders trespassing all over the place."

About a month went by after Romulus, Hugh, and Vernon stopped by Baylus Poteat's trailer to ask him for help in guarding the Andersons' family cemetery. Although Baylus had recently lost his leg to his diabetes, his sons were used to guard duty. Romulus was not certain if it was their daddy's influence or the marijuana they grew up protecting, but all of the Poteat boys seemed on edge. To talk to Baylus and his wife, you wouldn't identify them with such nervous offspring. Romulus thought maybe the boys absorbed too much of their parents' worries, the way one of Telitha's chocolate puddings once absorbed the smell of an onion she'd cut up and left beside the dessert.

During the month that Romulus and Telitha waited, they visited the cemetery at least twice a week. Every time they went, one of the Poteat boys, sometimes two or three, glided out from among the trees to speak to them. Telitha made a point out of taking something for the boys to eat. Romulus took them a half pint of Vernon's brew on a couple of visits. Then one Saturday morning, one of Baylus's boys knocked on Romulus's door.

"Daddy said for you to come over to the house." The boy leaned against the door frame with one hand. His other hand scratched above his kidney.

"Did you boys catch somebody in the cemetery?" Romulus was still wearing his old boots, the ones he put on when he went to feed the chickens.

"Daddy just said to tell you to come to the house." Finished scratching his back, the boy straightened up slightly, pulling his pants up on his hips. "Daddy said your wife mightn't be comfortable if she come with you, but if your granddaddy's home, he might ought to come."

As it turned out, Romulus had brought Vernon home the night before. On his way down to Vernon's basement, he picked up his brogans. If the old man had fired up his still, he wouldn't want to leave until the run was finished, but Romulus figured if Baylus was sending one of his sons out to deliver an invitation for a visit, then something had happened and nobody wanted to wait on an old man to finish cooking his corn.

As soon as Romulus saw that his grandfather was just stirring his mash, he sat down on the steps to change his shoes. "Don't fire up your boiler yet."

"You come to take a lesson?" Vernon tapped his wooden spoon against the side of his bucket.

"Baylus Poteat wants us to come and see him." Romulus worked his feet into his shoes without untying them.

"I guess I had better go with you. Seeing as how Baylus thinks you'll need me." Vernon leaned over and sniffed the mash. "I worry this mash will get overripe. Telitha has it timed just right. It needs to be run right now."

"I don't see any reason why you really need to be there." Romulus ran his finger along the top edge of his shoes, pausing here and there to pull up small folds of leather and straighten wrinkles in his socks.

"Let me just dump this mash in the pot and get it to cooking." Vernon lifted the bucket.

"We don't have time." Romulus walked over to his grandfather. The yeasty smell of the beer softened his impatience.

The old man had such bony arms; the two tendons of his scrawny neck quivered as he poured the mash into the modified pressure cooker. "I bet Baylus would appreciate tending to this business. Back before he turned to farming the weed, he tried more than once to buy our moonshine recipe."

"Maybe we ought to give it to him as a reward." Romulus tried not to watch his grandfather too closely.

"He couldn't have made it the same—even with the recipe." Vernon set the steel bucket down on the counter and gave it a half turn as if tightening it in place. "He's knowed that for a long time. Baylus works from a lot of wrong principles, but he ain't foolish." Vernon opened a cabinet door below the sink and pulled out a quart jar of moonshine, then a pint. "I know what Baylus wants."

Backing toward the stairs, Romulus watched Vernon clamp the lid on the pressure cooker. "Go ahead, fire it up." He hesitated, looking at the early morning sun pinging through all the chinks in the leaves of the trees along the lake, tingling life back into the numb water. "I'll tell Telitha to keep an eye on your kitchen."

Baylus's driveway was always in better shape than the gravel road that belonged to the state. People who knew Baylus also knew that the asphalt driveway had been a present to his wife, Chesney. If Baylus had followed his own inclinations, he would have let his driveway get as rough as the road up to Romulus's family cemetery. But Chesney drove a Mercury

Marquis, and she told everyone that she didn't plan to park her car in a mud hole every time she came home.

Romulus wasn't surprised to see that Chesney's Marquis wasn't parked in its usual place. However, he was disappointed not to see the large white van. He'd expected it to be in the driveway surrounded by Baylus's son's muddy Jeeps and pickups. All of Baylus's dogs crowded on the front porch in a subdued scramble to press their noses against the door. Three men who might have been Baylus's sons or friends of his sons slouched on the rails of the porch. They looked tired, but satisfied. They wore the expression that Romulus usually saw on men's faces who had a deer strapped on the hoods of their trucks.

"Just go on in." One of the men on the porch nodded at Romulus, but his eye strayed to the quart jar Vernon carried.

The thick air inside the trailer forced Romulus to take a step back, but before the delay was obvious, Vernon gave him a push from behind. In the center of the small living room squatted a coffee table where a vaporizer sat billowing out a cloud that smelled strongly of camphor. Closer to the floor throbbed an oilier, sweeter smell–kerosene.

On the other side of the coffee table sat the couch. Through the mist, Romulus saw two young men who were dressed for some kind of outdoor activity not native to Goshen Holler. They were dirty, but it was grime they had not antic-ipated–not the kind of dirt a man brought back in the house after he'd slopped hogs or worked on his furnace. These two boys hadn't earned the dirt on their faces and all over their clothes. It had been given to them.

Then Romulus realized that one reason the dirt looked out of place on the two boys was how pale both of them were. As his eyes adjusted to the dim light of Baylus's living room, Romulus also realized that some of the dirt was dried blood.

Nine or ten of Baylus's relatives crowded around the living room. They didn't speak a word, slouching and hanging back like vultures. Even before Vernon finished pulling the door shut behind him, the small ripple of disturbance he and Romulus created in the room had already settled back into a contemplation of the man who stretched out in his recliner next to the couch.

Baylus Poteat sat directly in front of the cloud puffing from the vaporizer. At any given moment, only part of Baylus was visible. One second, Romulus saw Baylus's bald head. Another second, all Romulus saw was a swollen torso. Another second all that seemed visible of Baylus was part of his hip and the thigh where his leg had been amputated. These parts kept shifting prominence, and because Baylus wasn't limited by a union of his appendages, he seemed to Romulus larger than life.

"Them's your trespassers." Baylus's voice was full of phlegm and pain, but still solid and heavy.

It made Romulus think of a pitchfork.

"I wanted you to see their faces . . . look up, you sons of bitches . . . so you'd know if they ever come around again." Baylus paused, letting Romulus and Vernon study the blank faces of the two men. "We took pictures before they got so dirty." Baylus shifted slightly, more to let the two men know he was talking to them directly than to get a better look at them. "You can be damned sure everybody in this county who you don't want to meet will know who you are, what you look like, where you live, and where your family lives." Baylus took a few wavering breaths. "If any little thing gives me a uncomfortable thought about letting you boys leave, don't think just because I live in a mobile home and got only one leg, I can't get to you."

Baylus raised slightly from his chair and stroked the stump of his thigh. "Diabetes is bad, boys. But if we have anymore trouble from you, I'm going to do to you what diabetes is done to me. Rest assured I'll take all my life's disappointments out on you in the process."

As soon as Baylus settled back into his recliner, two of his boys moved over to the couch and jerked up the thieves. In less than ten seconds, Romulus and Vernon stood by themselves in the living room with Baylus.

"Is that jar for me?" Now, Baylus's voice lost some of its hardness, and its ragged edge reminded Romulus of a pack of dogs and how their howls rose like pine trees at night.

Vernon moved into the vaporizer's cloud and handed the quart of moonshine to Baylus. "For preserving the integrity of the Goshen Holler dead."

"Oh lordy." Baylus gave the jar a weak shake then stared at the bubbles. "There ain't no integrity when somebody like me's supposed to preserve it."

"Well, you caught them that we asked you to." Romulus discovered that when he spoke, he could taste the camphor mist, but it contained another taste, something like silver that slid to the back of his throat.

"Yeah, we caught them." Baylus held the jar on his stomach. "But by the time the boys got up to the cemetery them two vampires had already loaded three-fourths of the tombstones into their van."

"Them tombstones didn't get away, did they?" Romulus wondered if Baylus had underestimated the thieves in some way, maybe miscounted or neglected to watch while another thief slipped into the driver's seat and thundered out of the county.

"Them tombstones is still up in your cemetery." Baylus sat up as straight as he could. "They ain't in the right places, though. They're stacked five high in the back of that van. You got a problem if you ain't got some kind of diagram that tells you the names of the people whose stones been pulled up."

Very clearly, Romulus pictured in his mind the cemetery, some of the graves old enough to have gone back to plain ground. All that he'd have to go by were the shallow holes left where the stones had been pulled out. He could imagine the gaps, at least sixty if Baylus was right in his estimations. . . sixty empty places over relatives he never knew. For a moment, he wondered if the buried would mind having the wrong markers over their heads.

"We ain't got no problems." Vernon produced his pint jar. "You just lend us two or three boys to help us set the stones. I'll tell them where they go. I remember them all."

He gave the pint jar a shake. "Them beautiful beads. Proof this pure preserves the memory." Vernon studied the bubbles as if he had names for each one. Then he unscrewed the lid.

"Pass that over to me when you're done." Romulus moved closer to his grandfather.

Nectars of the Wild

Camellia spent most of the morning getting her hands bloody from the blackberry vines. Very deliberately, she had been plunging her hands into the tightest tangles, places so dense that blackberries had no room to grow.

Ten or fifteen yards below her, another woman stooped over the blackberry thicket. Ava Bradshaw, for the first time in the five years that she and Camellia had begun picking berries on this hill that rose up to support a small cemetery, had filled her bucket almost as full as Camellia's because she could concentrate on the berries and the thorns.

Each scratch on Camellia's hand represented a swipe her conscience made at her for committing adultery with Ava's husband, Malcolm. She looked forward to getting home and drenching her hands with rubbing alcohol. The burn would make her more sorry, but it wouldn't make things right. In a way, Camellia wished she had been given Malcolm's punishment. Then again, just being there to see what happened to him had convinced Camellia that she would never cheat on her husband again.

Straightening up, Camellia had to brace her spine with the heels of her palms dug into her hips. She was only twenty-two, but berry picking always added fifty years to her age.

For a couple of seconds, Camellia wished she **was** seventy. Maybe by then, she'd be clear of fleshly desires. On the other hand, she'd also be closer to dying, and she wasn't ready for that—yet. Especially not with this adultery to work out of her soul. She squatted back down, ready to submit once more to the thorns.

"You want to quit before it gets too hot?" Ava's voice was smooth, concerned. She often spoke to Camellia like a mother rather than like a neighbor and business partner.

She and Camellia ran a small roadside stand selling jams and jellies which they canned themselves. They also sold the honey that Malcolm collected from his bee hives. Of course, Malcolm was only a part-time bee keeper. Most of the time, he worked as the head dispatcher for Hudson Freight Lines—the same company that Camellia's husband, Dwight Marley, drove for.

In fact, Dwight had known Malcolm before he had known Camellia. They had started working for Hudson Freight at the same time, twelve years ago. Malcolm, though, had started out in the office while Dwight started out in a truck. That was seven years before Camellia and Dwight got together. Malcolm had gone to college. Camellia wondered if that's why he always stayed so neat and slim. She suspected that no matter what some boys studied, they all learned how to take care of themselves.

Dwight, on the other hand, seemed to collect a quarter pound with every over-the-road mile he drove. When she had this thought, Camellia forced herself to slowly grasp the thorniest vine she could find and squeeze it until tears came to her eyes.

Dwight was a much better husband than she was a wife. His fat was no sin—or it was his only sin. And he didn't deliberately put on weight. Certainly not the way she had deliberately signaled to Malcolm that she needed his company up at her Aunt Corley's old ramshackle house.

Glancing over her shoulder at Ava, Camellia gripped the thorns even tighter. Then she realized that all of these deep scratches on her hands would certainly make Ava wonder what was wrong. Quiet as Ava was, Camellia was certain that her friend was always keeping her eyes open. Why hadn't she thought about that before she and Malcolm put their heads together and schemed to get Dwight and Ava out of town at the same time so they could sneak up to that old house? Surely Ava already knew that something was going on–even if it was already over after just one night.

Something had to be done to throw Ava off the track. Camellia checked her plastic bucket. She'd filled the thing over thirty minutes ago, before she decided to cut up her hands to make her soul feel better. Making as big a show as possible about standing up and straightening her back, Camellia turned around, awkwardly wiping her forehead with her arm. "Ava?" She caught sight of Ava standing up. Not giving her friend a chance to speak, Camellia took a step toward Ava, easily hooked her toe in a thick knot of blackberry vines, and allowed herself to pitch forward into the dark green leaves, the deep purple berries, and the punishing thorns.

"Good Lord, Camellia!" Ava shouted.

The pain in her hands and along her arms came as no surprise to Camellia. It'd have to hurt to be convincing. What she hadn't expected was the pain in her chest and stomach. It was so sharp and satisfying that for a moment, she thought about just rolling all the way down the steep hill through the blackberry vines until she was permanently scarred and stained with blackberry juice and her own blood. Maybe she could stir up a snake or two on her trip.

What helped her control the impulse to do as much damage to herself as possible was the thought of all those people staring at her when she went to the mall. Or how the people who stopped to buy her and Ava's jams would look at her like she was another hillbilly who'd been mauled by a bear or her husband. So Camellia let herself rock across the thorns two or three times, but she didn't let loose her grip on the side of the hill.

Much quicker than she expected, she felt Ava's hands on her shoulders, pulling her up out of the bushes, each thorn giving her one final little nip goodbye. "Did you faint, Camellia?"

With no effort, Ava rolled Camellia off of the vines while lifting her torso up onto her lap. Kind as she was, Ava had never struck Camellia as the woman to be married to Malcolm. She had been in college for a year. That's where she met Malcolm. But then she'd decided that she didn't like school. She'd started working at the college cafeteria so she could be close to Malcolm. She'd told Camellia that she was smart enough to go to college to find her husband, but she'd never really been interested in learning more than she already knew about putting up fruits and vegetables.

Camellia pulled herself up out of Ava's lap. "I didn't faint. I just stood up too quick and when I went to take a step, I got my toe hung up in one of them blamed bushes."

"Look at what you did to your hands." Ava grabbed one of Camellia's wrists and studied first the back and then the palm of her hand. "You just about shredded your skin."

"Nobody'll notice. Not Dwight anyhow. All he can think about is that lost goat of his." As quickly as possible, Camellia wanted Ava to channel her sympathy over in Dwight's direction. For close to three months now, he'd been opining over his goat, Casper. At different times, she, Ava, and Malcolm had wandered all over the county helping look for the animal.

It had been during the hunt for Casper, late one evening, back when he'd first disappeared and Camellia hadn't gotten fed up with Dwight wanting to go out every evening after supper to look and look that she had found herself walking through a grove of trees with Malcolm. Dwight had tracked off down toward a creek, so intent on finding goat tracks in the sandy ground that he hadn't paid any attention to his wife and best friend, standing on the path just watching him tromp through the high grass.

Before leaving the house, Dwight had promised them that they wouldn't have to get off the path and wade through the heavy dew. So Camellia had kept on the sandals she was wearing, and Malcolm had not changed out of his canvas deck shoes. When Dwight had split off from the path and gone into the tall wet grass, Camellia and Malcolm had simply stood and watched until he disappeared.

As soon as Dwight was out of sight, Camellia grew aware of Malcolm's after shave. It was called Islander. Ava bought it through her Avon lady. Maybe it did smell like palm trees and blue ocean, but what most impressed Camellia was the fact that Malcolm was wearing after shave so late in the evening. She knew he and Ava weren't going out because Ava was in her kitchen–and would be in her kitchen for the next six or seven hours–keeping watch over the thirty pints of strawberry preserves she was boiling out.

Dwight was as good as anybody Camellia knew to keep himself clean, but especially when he had nowhere to go, he'd take a bath and that was it. In no time at all, he smelled like a man who had no plans–except maybe to go out and look for his goat.

That was what made Malcolm different: he never seemed to let the day wear down on him. Camellia imagined that just sitting on a couch beside a man like Malcolm could be as exciting as sitting on a jet waiting to land in Atlanta or Miami. Being at college was probably what gave Malcolm that slight buzz to his outline, as if simply by tightening his stomach muscles, he could transform the dullest evening to a Friday or Saturday night when they had tickets to an ALABAMA concert at the Charlotte Coliseum.

Yearning for the kind of date she had never known when she was younger, Camellia had swayed against Malcolm while folding her arms over her chest and staring at the darkening spot where her husband had dwindled away. When she felt a slight sway from Malcolm in her direction, Camellia had leaned a little harder, her shoulder then her arm then her elbow slowly pressing against Malcolm's. After a few seconds, Malcolm had slid his arm around Camellia's waist.

If Malcolm had been Dwight, he would have kept his arm right there around her waist. But Camellia, almost certain she could hear a faint hum from her own skin and Malcolm's, nearly shuddered when Malcolm's hand drifted slightly below her waist, down to the roundest part of her hip. Malcolm didn't make the mistake of sliding his hand back to rub her butt. She'd have known him for a dog if he'd done that. But putting his hand on her hip–that widest part–let her know that he saw her, could see her as much more than just his wife's best friend.

For barely a second, he applied the slightest pressure to her hip, pulling her against him. It was almost as if he had kissed her but not wetly or hungrily or selfishly. "Rightly" was all Camellia could think of at the moment: sunset, cool woods all around, her husband off hunting for a lost goat, Ava sweating over steaming jars of strawberry mash, and Malcolm smelling like a new suit and a marble elevator to the penthouse.

All the pleasures of the world seemed stored in Malcolm that night. He was a hive and each cell of his body contained a drop of forbidden honey which made Camellia's body ache sweetly, as if adultery would tone her muscles. Even as she put her arm, low, around Malcolm's waist and returned his pressure, she knew she wasn't clear in her head, but the confusion and the guilt at that point were part of the attraction—like the chewy little wax walls which held the honey.

Down the narrow path leading off the hill and through the cow pasture which sat across the road from Ava's house, Camellia watched her friend. A suspicious person always walked differently from someone who thought the world was what it seemed. Suspicion made you stiff, from what Camellia had observed. Since that night in the woods almost two months ago, Camellia had watched Ava closely. No matter how smart Ava might be, she wouldn't be able to hide her suspicion because she was a woman who flowed everywhere. The minute she got a solid suspicion in her walk, Camellia would know it just as surely as if Ava had started wearing a cast on her leg.

So far, Ava continued to move as smoothly as always. In the one conversation Camellia'd had with Malcolm since their night in the same bed, he'd assured her that Ava had believed his story about all the tiny bites he'd brought home with him. He'd told her that his bees had turned on him. A part of her that she'd desperately wanted to outgrow had told her that sin always left its marks one way or another. The thought that made Camellia stop in the middle of the path and bite her lip was that Ava might have seen those bites for what they were and had simply been good enough to let them be Malcolm's and Camellia's punishment. That kind of forgiveness scraped Camellia deeper than any of the blackberry briars had.

"Come on in the house and let me put some salve on them cuts of yours." Ava waited for Camellia beside the road.

For the time being, the last place Camellia wanted to spend time was in Ava's house. It was hard enough after that Saturday night with Malcolm in her Aunt Corley's to go into her own house. It had been Dwight's grandparents' house, back when they were still able to live alone and raise their corn, cabbage, and tobacco. In addition to the barn, the house had at least a dozen other outbuildings of varying sizes. Camellia stayed away from them because Dwight had warned her that given the right weather conditions and a strong enough wind, they might all fall over at once one day.

Actually, when one of the older tobacco curing sheds did fall over, Dwight and Malcolm had built the roadside stand from which Camellia and Ava had been selling their nectars of the wild.

"Ava, I'm going on home so I can just wash myself all over." Camellia handed Ava her bucket of blackberries. "I feel like I got mites crawling where they've never been before."

"I'd want to get clean too." Ava lifted both buckets as if determining how many pint jars she'd have to scald. "But be sure you put something on them hands."

Camellia nodded. "You won't have much canning to do with that little mess."

"Don't have much time for canning today anyway. Malcolm wants to go skiing when he comes home from work." Ava turned to go up the gravel walkway to her house, a broad brick ranch house surrounded by box shrubs. "Why don't you and Dwight come with us? We don't need to keep the stand open every minute."

Her first impulse was to avoid any situation where she'd have to be near Malcolm–especially with him in his bathing suit–especially in the company of Ava and Dwight. Besides, Ava knew that Dwight didn't care for wobbling around in Malcolm's ski boat, roasting those parts of his body he didn't cover up with towels and sweat shirts. Camellia didn't want to make him uncomfortable after he'd spent most of the morning propped up against the wall of the roadside stand while his wife and neighbor went out to pick blackberries. Rather than trying to get him to do something he didn't enjoy, Camellia thought she ought to be busy being nicer to Dwight.

Then she realized that several weeks had gone by since she'd forced Dwight to go somewhere he didn't want to go. Ava probably knew that. Ava also knew how much Camellia liked being out on Malcolm's boat. For a sickening second, Camellia wondered if perhaps Ava hadn't already contacted Dwight and worked out this little trip to test Malcolm and her. Briefly, Camellia's indignation overshadowed her guilt. Why did Ava have to resort to conniving with Dwight? They'd all feel much cleaner if Ava just came out and accused her.

"I'll see if I can talk Dwight into it." Camellia studied Ava's face. All she saw was a faint smile that could have meant anything because Ava was prone to smiling even when one of her pots of preserves turned too thick to sell.

"After that long trip he got back from, I'd think he'd enjoy rocking away a few hours on the river." Ava rocked sideways a couple of times to emphasize her point.

"Maybe if we'd put a fishing pole in his hand he'd be happy. But you know how he feels about skiing." Camellia shrugged.

"Well, don't let him talk you into looking for that goat the rest of the afternoon."

Standing there at the edge of Ava's front yard, Camellia could see the tin roof of their roadside stand where her husband waited for her. He was one of the best people she knew when it came to waiting. Malcolm was the one who said that Dwight's metabolism probably made him so good at waiting, probably made him such a good long distance truck driver. He never got in a hurry, never acted like he ought to be somewhere except right where he stood or sat or propped against a wall, reading some book or pamphlet.

Besides being big and attached to wherever he stood or sat, Dwight entertained himself by reading. If he read detective novels or horror stories, Camellia would have been more comfortable with her husband, but she just never knew what Dwight might pull out of his pocket. He was always collecting reading material from the oddest places: drug store counters, tourist information centers, restaurant bulletin boards, people on street corners, people standing at the top of highway exit ramps, door-to-door campaigners, filling station bathrooms, truckstop leaflet racks, doctors' offices, clinic tables, gun shows, car shows, tire stores, and from hitchhikers he'd pick up on the interstate.

Maybe if all of his reading made some kind of difference in the kind of man Dwight was, Camellia reasoned, she wouldn't have let her affections stray, but Dwight was more like himself now five years later than he was when they first got married. Camellia could tell by the way Dwight was mooning after his goat.

It had been a wedding present from some of the other truckers. Camellia admitted to herself that the goat had been cute. In fact, she was the one who had named it Casper because of its luminescent gray fur and the gray marks which made it look like it had the vague image of a human face stenciled over its goat face.

Still, Camellia never let herself get attached to Casper. Until Dwight could fix up one of the outbuildings for the goat's house, he had kept it staked outside their bedroom window at night. Camellia had never been around goats before that night, and the sound it made kept her from ever falling completely asleep. When it baaaaed, all that Camellia could think about was a skeleton pulling a guitar string up and down its back. That vision had come to her the first night that she and Dwight slept together as man and wife. Maybe that was why she found herself breaking her vows. She imagined trying to explain her infidelity to Dwight or Ava by blaming the goat. Better to let them think the wrong thoughts than let them see that deep into her mind.

Of course, she had seen from the very first day of the goat's disappearance that deep down, Dwight was suspicious of her, and maybe even Malcolm—not about adultery but about Casper. Dwight knew that Camellia didn't like Casper. As the goat had grown older, his temper had—like his wool—coarsened. More than once, he had chased Camellia out of his little shed because she had filled his water tank crooked or poured his feed too noisily or something. She tried to explain that Casper behaved the way he did because Dwight stayed on the road so much. The goat felt neglected.

Given the chance, though, Malcolm would have run the goat out of the county. After a day or two, when Casper realized that Dwight had gone off on another trip, the goat always decided he needed to do a little traveling himself. Up until his final disappearance, Casper limited his explorations to Malcolm's garden or hedges. However, the goat's most destructive visits took him into the field behind Malcolm and Ava's house where Malcolm kept his bee hives. Several times, Casper had knocked over one of the small white boxes that contained the bees and eaten what he could of the honey and the comb. Although Malcolm had refused to take the money Dwight offered him, he often asked Dwight when he was going to get rid of that goat.

Dwight was one of those people, though, who didn't let what people said bother him, even when people really wanted him to be bothered. If he had been more botherable, Camellia thought maybe he would have been more interesting. She caught herself. She could see that she was just trying to make excuses for herself. Showed just how low she had slipped, holding a man's agreeable nature against him.

Then again, it was that agreeable nature that allowed her and Malcolm to sneak off. Almost like Dwight wanted to give them the chance to commit adultery. That was what made Camellia so angry about Dwight. If you just let something happen, you weren't entirely free from blame. Given that line of argument, Camellia admitted to herself, that she probably was responsible for the goat disappearing. She had gone for three days without checking on him, without making sure his water tank was filled. He was sensitive to that kind of neglect, even though he had a stream not two hundred yards from his shed and if he really got thirsty, all he had to do was bounce down the hill. But she and Ava had been worked to death getting the strawberries picked and preserved that whole month.

To her credit, Camellia had been the one who had saved the goat on more than one occasion when he had climbed up in the rafters of the old barn and then not been able to climb back down. Nobody had told her that goats could climb the way they did. All Casper needed was a ledge four inches wide, and he'd go as high as the roof. Naturally, when he first disappeared, Camellia had looked up at all the beams in the barn behind the house. She had just assumed that Dwight would have checked all the other outbuildings. Now that she thought about it, she didn't remember Dwight saying anything about looking in any of those derelict buildings. If she offered to help him search the buildings, she might be able to trade some goat search time for some water skiing time.

Ava and Camellia's roadside stand was a miniature log cabin about ten feet by ten feet with three open air windows that ran the entire length of the sides and front of the cabin. The shutters could be raised all the way up or lowered half way down and hooked with a chain to serve as awnings when the weather was too bright or rainy. The idea for the awnings had been Malcolm's but Dwight was the one who built them. From the floor to the ceiling, shelves of jelly and jam crowded the inside of the cabin and forced customers to move around as if their ankles were tied. Camellia had once told Ava that people acted reverent when they were surrounded by jars of jelly. Ava had replied that she didn't care how they acted as long as they bought something before they left.

Comments like that made Camellia understand why Malcolm would betray Ava. Being practical was a lot like being easy to please. But wasn't being practical and being easy to please real close to being self-satisfied? And wasn't being self-satisfied a whole lot like being vain? Camellia nodded to herself. This mess wasn't entirely her fault. Not the goat—not the adultery. She didn't sleep with Malcolm just because she wanted to be bad. In a way, she was trying to improve herself . . . or her life. She wanted to know what was on the other side of being a good wife.

She didn't like what she had seen. And she knew that Malcolm had learned his lesson too.

As Camellia had expected, Dwight was in exactly the same position she'd left him in three hours earlier—resting in a ladder back chair with his thick legs spraddled on each side of the chair, tilted against the front of the little cabin. He was still reading a slick-looking little pamphlet entitled NEW AGE FIRST AID which he said he picked up in a grocery store in Boulder, Colorado.

"Did you sell anything?" Camellia kept her hands behind her back. She didn't feel up to explaining how she got her arms and hands scratched. Even when she wasn't guilty of adultery, Camellia had trouble explaining anything to Dwight. He always wanted to know more. If he pushed her too hard today, she worried she would tell him too much.

"Traffic's been kind of light." Heavily, but with obvious concern for the slender chair, Dwight lowered himself to the ground. "But I did sell four jars of the strawberry jam." Dwight smiled up at Camellia and dogeared the page he was reading.

Camellia leaned her shoulder against the door frame, still keeping her hands behind her back. "Ava asked us to go skiing with her and Malcolm."

"I thought you told me that Malcolm got stung all over by his bees." Dwight slumped, tapping his leg with the pamphlet.

"Skiing'll help take his mind off the itching. Maybe the sun'll evaporate some of the poison." Camellia unhitched the shutter on the side of the cabin and lowered it, closing off the window. She wanted Dwight to see that she was serious about getting away from the jelly business for the afternoon. "What's that word for burning when you do it to kill the germs?" She knew that Dwight liked to be asked for help.

"Cauterize?" Dwight stood up and placed the chair inside the cabin.

"Yes." Camellia padlocked the shutter she'd just closed. "Getting out in the sun on a pair of skis might help Malcolm cauterize his bee stings."

"I think he'd have to have open wounds to really be cauterized." Dwight lowered the shutter on the other side of the cabin.

"Well, a bee sting is a little open wound, ain't it?" Camellia tossed Dwight a padlock.

"I guess so." Dwight turned his head toward Camellia, but his eyes, when he blinked, came out staring in different directions, a sign that he was weighing the accuracy of what she said. "But from what I've read, I wouldn't think the sun would be good for any kind of skin poisoning." He turned his attention to fitting the padlock through the brackets on the window and the side of the cabin.

"I always heard sunlight helped evaporate the poison and dry out the festering." Camellia closed the shutter at the front of the cabin.

"Lord! Malcolm's not festering, is he?" Dwight propped his forearm against the corner of the cabin and leaned toward Camellia. It was a pose that emphasized how far his pants hung below his belly.

"Not as far as I know. I've not seen him today. He's at work." Camellia had to jiggle this shutter to get the brackets aligned. She was glad she didn't have to look her husband in the eye. She could be critical all she wanted to about his weight, but she knew she had years of making up to do. After what happened to Malcolm, she was convinced that sex sins were punished in ways she couldn't imagine until she had seen it.

Looking back, Camellia wondered why she and Malcolm hadn't just driven down to Hickory or some other good-sized town and rented a motel room like all the other people who committed adultery. But no, she thought she'd have more courage if she took Malcolm up to her Aunt Corey's house. In the back of her mind, she figured if either she or Malcolm backed out at the last minute, they could pretend that they really had come up to see if the old house might be restored and sold to some of the Florida people who were always looking for summer homes in the mountains.

When Camellia caught her first glimpse of the house so heavily overgrown, she came close to suggesting that they not even look at the inside. Several gnarled apple trees crowded up against the house, waist-high weeds reached up past the lower windowpanes. Malcolm walked in front of Camellia, beating the thistles and the milkweed back with the shotgun he'd brought along for protection.

At the time, the gun made Malcolm seem dangerous and exciting. Certainly, Dwight had his own collection of guns. Every truck driver whom Camellia had met carried some kind of gun with him. But as she watched Malcolm batting at the weeds with the gun, she realized that probably neither one of them thought they might need protection against Dwight. Camellia was shocked by the depth of the chill when she imagined Malcolm pointing that gun at Dwight.

Before she could feel too guilty about putting her husband in that kind of danger, she reassured herself with the certain knowledge that Dwight was in Boulder that very night. He had called her not long after she'd gotten her call from Malcolm letting her know that he'd returned from delivering Ava to her mother's house. Then they had driven up to Aunt Corley's house in separate cars, just in case somebody stopped by their homes in Hibriten.

Despite how overgrown the outside of the house was, Camellia was relieved to find the inside of the house pretty livable. Because the house had no electricity or water, they had brought lanterns, water, and a portable chemical toilet. Malcolm liked to anticipate every possible source of discomfort. First, Camellia and Malcolm checked all of the eight rooms of the house to make sure no large wild animals had moved in. Then while Malcolm set up his Coleman four-burner gas stove in the kitchen, Camellia beat the dust out of the bed in the master bedroom and tried not to choke on her own heart.

In the red and pink light of the sun going down behind Spruce Mountain, Camellia took off her clothes and waited for Malcolm. Like most men, Camellia suspected, Malcolm looked better with a few clothes on. He wasn't just slim, he was skinny. He was bony. And when he got on top of her she kept feeling prodded by his joints which seemed to have surprisingly sharp edges. The room was stuffy; Camellia felt bruised. She was disappointed to discover that just because something was wrong still didn't make it fun on the first try.

Maybe because of the stuffiness or because of the long day both she and Malcolm had worked through, they fell asleep. Camellia knew she hadn't meant to fall asleep because she always had to sleep on the side closest to a wall. For some reason, on that evening of their adultery, Malcolm had the side next to the wall. They must have slept for nearly two hours because when Malcolm woke Camellia up, it was dark outside. Later, when Camellia had time to check her watch, it was eight-thirty.

What woke her was Malcolm bumping her, not like a lover, but like a man uncomfortable all by himself. At first, he shuffled back and forth on his side of the bed. Soon, he was twisting all over the place, bumping into Camellia and grinding his teeth.

"What's wrong with you?" Camellia had asked, trying to touch Malcolm but frightened by his thrashing.

"Get me some light!" Malcolm suddenly grew still.

From the way the bed groaned and the mattress tilted, Camellia knew that he had stood up in the bed. He made a noise under his breath, a thin hum unraveling just behind his nose.

All the time that Camellia fumbled with the lantern, she heard that frail hum which she realized was a stifled moan just as she lit the wick. What she first thought when she held the lantern over the bed where Malcolm still stood, his arms and legs spread, was that he had somehow changed colors. He was a dark brown—not just his usual golden tan, but brown like an acorn.

While Camellia stood with her mouth hanging open and the lantern stretched toward Malcolm, he had slowly reached down and pulled off a patch of his brown skin. He was his regular color underneath. For a second, he examined the membrane he had pulled from his stomach, but from where Camellia stood, the brown seemed to dissolve, running through Malcolm's fingers and down his wrist.

"Ticks!" He brushed and slapped at his sides, his stomach, his chest, flipping whole handfuls of ticks all over the room.

Camellia had never seen anyone covered with ticks before. From a crack in the paneling next to Malcolm's side of the bed, she could see a dark stain running down the wall and along the bed. The ticks had oozed out of the wall into the bed and just stopped at Malcolm's body like he was a human dam.

Momentarily leaving Malcolm in the dark, Camellia jumped back from the bed and held the lantern close to her own body. Her skin was crawling, but she didn't have any ticks on her.

When Malcolm had almost exhausted himself trying to beat the ticks off his body, Camellia had shouted to him to come out on the porch where she doused him with the two gallons of kerosene they had brought for the lanterns and the stove. Then she had tried to rinse him off with the ten gallons of water they'd brought along, but he still smelled highly combustible.

When she finished locking the door of the cabin, Camellia turned to Dwight and rubbed his upper arm. "I'll make a deal with you. Be sweet and go skiing this afternoon, and when we get back, I'll help you hunt for Casper."

Dwight patted her hand. "I've about give up on finding him. I had a lot of time to think on the trip out to Boulder. And if I've not come across him in three months, I'm not likely ever to come across him."

As she walked beside Dwight toward their house, she rested her hand on his shoulder. "I had a thought while I was picking blackberries. Did you look up in the rafters of all the outbuildings when you looked for Casper? He liked to climb the support beams, you know."

"We could go look right now." Dwight moved sideways, bumping into Camellia. "Only three or four of them outbuildings got rafters that would have interested Casper."

Camellia grabbed Dwight's wrist. "I want to go home and take a bath." She held up her scratched hands. "I fell in the blackberry vines."

Seeing her injury, Dwight had no room to argue. He followed her the rest of the way home, and while she was bathing, she knew he was digging around in his drawers to find the baggy pants and sweatshirt he always wore when everyone else was wearing a bathing suit.

Not long after Camellia put on her bathing suit and poured rubbing alcohol over her hands and arms, Malcolm and Ava pulled into their driveway in Malcolm's extended bed Dodge Ram. The ski boat he pulled was the same metal flake candy-apple red as his truck. From ten feet away, as Malcolm and Ava approached her kitchen door on the carport, Camellia could tell that Malcolm's tick bites were worse than they had been. All of the places had turned into red mounds. He looked as if he weighed fifteen pounds more than he usually did–all of it bug bite weight.

"Is that you, Malcolm?" Dwight pushed up behind Camellia. Whenever she wore her bathing suit, Dwight always wanted to rub up against her.

"Me and my bee stings." Malcolm held his arms up in the air and then pulled up his tank top to show the bites all over his chest and stomach.

"How do you stand it?" Dwight stepped outside the door and took a closer look at Malcolm.

"Just try to keep my mind on other things. Like skiing." Malcolm lowered his shirttail.

Dwight shook his head. "What'd you do to piss off them bees?"

"All I can figure is they must have found out that I hang around truck drivers most of the day." Malcolm rolled his eyes from Ava to Camellia.

"I told Camellia that you ought to stay out of the sun." Dwight let his gaze drift from Malcolm to his boat.

Malcolm followed Dwight's gaze. "No. No. What I need is some activity."

"Well, I think your first activity will be fitting all four of us into the cab of your truck." Dwight followed Ava and Malcolm inside his house.

"I'll just sit on your lap," Camellia said to Dwight as she handed Malcolm a cooler.

"Did you go to the doctor yet?" Dwight gave Camellia a happy nod as he picked up a larger cooler and went out behind Malcolm.

"Do them bites worry you, Ava?" Camellia looked around the kitchen to make sure she hadn't forgotten anything. She picked up the towels she'd laid out for her and Dwight. His was dark blue with a green Peterbilt truck roaring down a highway. Hers was a deep pink with a desert scene. Dwight had brought them home a couple of summers earlier from another trip he'd made out to Colorado.

"They did when I first got home from Mama's and saw him all lumpy. But I figure if they didn't kill him last night, they're not going to kill him at all." Ava adjusted the strap of her bathing suit and moved toward the kitchen door.

Since Camellia had known Ava, she thought she was too casual. Oh, at first, you liked someone who didn't seem to take anything but canning berries seriously. Then one day, you realized that Ava was maybe too casual about you, like maybe you didn't matter as much to her as you thought you should. And after that, you started feeling as if you could be more casual about her. Being too casual was like giving somebody permission to do whatever she wanted.

But Camellia didn't know why she was still trying to blame somebody else for her adultery. Except she wanted to know why Malcolm had been punished and she hadn't. If she hadn't leaned up against him on the path in the woods that evening, he wouldn't have known what she wanted. What she wanted now was a more definite punishment. Until then, she was going to feel a little bit like one of Ava's bathing suits which never quite fit her.

When they got to the boat ramp at the river, Malcolm asked everybody to get out. With everybody crowded in the front seat, he didn't have the room he needed to concentrate on backing the long boat down into the water. Even with Ava, Camellia, and Dwight standing beside the gravel road that led down into the water, Malcolm had trouble backing the trailer.

"Must be his bee stings are interfering with his backing." Dwight crossed his arms over his stomach and blew air from between his lips as Malcolm tried for the third time to get the boat lined up on the ramp.

"I've never seen him have this kind of trouble before." Ava shaded her eyes with her palm and peered at the truck as if to make sure her husband was the man in the driver's seat.

This was it, Camellia realized. They wouldn't be discovered by Ava and Dwight sneaking up on them like she expected. It would be something stupid that would give them away, not only reveal their guilt but humiliate them in the process, so people would say, "Well, what do you expect from a couple of stupid people like Camellia and Malcolm?" She admitted to herself that she expected a college graduate to hold up a little better to the guilt or the tick bites than Malcolm seemed to be.

Any second, she expected Dwight to go over to the truck and drag Malcolm out of the seat. That would be Malcolm's signal to confess everything. And there she would stand in her two piece yellow bathing suit more guilty and stupid than she'd ever felt in her life.

Finally, Malcolm got the boat trailer on the ramp and backed down into the water. As soon as Dwight saw the trailer roll between the two poles showing where the ramp's edges disappeared into the water, he trotted down into the water and began unfastening the cargo straps. Camellia knew that Dwight could have gotten the boat lined up on the ramp on the first try. Even on a bad day, Dwight backed better than any man she knew.

Where Dwight had trouble was getting into the boat. While Malcolm backed the boat away from the loading zone, Dwight parked the truck, the trailer rattling like a stool pigeon over the ruts in the parking lot. Camellia and Ava carried the coolers over to the water's edge and waited for Malcolm to make all the necessary adjustments to fuel lines, throttle controls, and ski equipment. He pulled the boat up as close to the bank as he could, but because the river bottom was slick and steep, Camellia and Ava were up to their waists in the water when they waded out to the boat with the coolers.

Slightly envious, Camellia watched as Ava, holding onto Malcolm's bumpy hand slid smoothly into the boat. She pushed her hair out of her face and looked up at Malcolm. His expression was as slick as the river bottom she felt under her feet. The closer she got to Malcolm, the harder it was to tell he'd done anything wrong. Had he learned that trick in college? Camellia wondered as she took his bumpy hand in her scratched one. Then she bobbed down, water rising to her shoulders, and pushed herself up, feeling Malcolm's pull on her arm, across her shoulders, and she rose from the water, hooked her leg over the side of the boat, gave a turn to her hips, and was standing in the boat, facing the bank where Dwight was just sloshing into the water.

This was probably what he disliked most about riding in Malcolm's boat—trying to get in. A quarter of a mile up the river was a dock. Malcolm had once suggested that Dwight walk up there and he could just step into the boat without all the struggle they had to go through trying to get him out of the river into the boat. But Camellia knew how Dwight would feel as he walked along the bank to the dock, like he was handicapped. Of course, if he felt that way, it was his own fault. He didn't have to stop and eat breakfast at every grill along the road. His lack of control was just as bad as Ava's casualness. It led Camellia into frustration and made her soft for temptation . . .

To clear her mind, Camellia leaned over the side of the boat next to Malcolm—careful not to brush up against his lumpy skin—and took the other hand that Dwight was waving above his head. As she expected, on the first three tries, Dwight thrashed in the water, his muscles knotting under the fat of his arms, but useless against his weight and the suction of the river. Then out of some desperate effort which threatened to tear off trim and scrape the fiberglass, Dwight finally managed to scramble and flop his way into the boat. For several seconds, Camellia, Malcolm, and Dwight hung over the side, catching their breath.

This time of the afternoon, the Catawba River was placid and green, stretching up the valley all the way to the Blue Ridge Mountains. It smelled faintly of fish and gasoline, but having grown up with the odor, Camellia felt calm blossoming to excitement as Malcolm chugged the boat around to face upriver, then opened the throttle, bringing the nose of the boat about thirty-five degrees out of the water while a spray fanned up along both sides of the boat, spreading two miniature rainbows over Camellia's and Ava's shoulders.

"Who wants to go first?" Malcolm shouted over the sizzle of the spray and the deep buzz of the motor.

What Camellia disliked most about skiing was having to sit in the water, waiting for the slack to pull out of the ski line. The deep green water had always made her uncomfortable even though she had a ski vest around her and a big boat tied to the other end of the rope. Today, the idea of sitting in that green water while her husband sped away from her in the company of Malcolm and Ava nearly strangled Camellia.

"You go on ahead, Ava." Camellia leaned over and tapped Ava's knee.

"Not in the mood yet." Ava pulled at her suit under her armpits. "I don't know if this suit'll stay on in fast water."

Malcolm looked over his shoulder at Dwight. "You want to give it a try?"

Dwight held his fingertips in the spray thrown up by the boat. "Maybe someday when I don't have good sense."

Cutting the throttle back, Malcolm slid from the driver's seat and picked up his neon orange vest from the floor beside him. "Ava get up here and drive."

Dwight shifted around on his bench seat until he was facing backwards. Camellia moved to the back of the boat so she could be Malcolm's official watcher. Up until today, she thought Malcolm on skis was one of the most breathtaking sights in the whole county. Today, for the first time, she noticed how prominent his knuckles were, how knotty all of his joints looked. He had a cocky way of latching his ski vest that made Camellia wonder if he had already forgotten about sleeping with her. Nobody was letting on that anything had happened. All of the air on the river felt dull green and oppressive to her.

They had pulled Malcolm for what seemed like miles when Camellia saw him hold his fist up over his head and point off to his right. Camellia looked in the direction he was pointing and saw the old Catawba Ski Club sign. Back when the club had been in operation, Malcolm had been a member, but not enough people in Hibriten cared about jumping to keep such a club alive. Several of the jump ramps still floated in the river and were kept in repair by a few daredevils, but since Camellia had been coming to the river with Malcolm and Ava, she'd never seen Malcolm jump, although he often talked about teaching her and Ava how to do it.

"Ava!" Camellia yelled. "Malcolm's trying to tell you something."

Ava twisted in the seat so she could get a better look at her husband. "He wants me to run him up a ramp." She made a slow turn away from one of the ramps and circled around so she could get a little closer to Malcolm. "You want to jump?" She pointed at the ramp.

Malcolm nodded vigorously and gave her the O.K. with his fingers. Ava opened the throttle a little further and headed down the river to get a running start.

"You going to let him try it?" Dwight slid backwards on his seat to get closer to Ava.

"Jumping is like riding a bicycle." Ava opened the throttle a little wider. "Besides, if he falls, he's got the whole river to catch him. He's never missed yet."

"The jump or the river?" Dwight pulled himself more erect, watching Malcolm then the approaching ramp.

"What made him want to try the jump?" Camellia turned to see if she could catch something in Ava's eyes, but her friend was too busy maneuvering the boat.

"Used to be the only time he jumped was when he needed to prove his manhood." Ava sped past the ramp and glanced back at Malcolm who was drifting over toward the ramp. He crouched slightly, anticipating the thump the skis would make when they slammed into the wooden ramp.

"Something's up at the top of that ramp." Dwight jumped to his feet, craning his neck. "Something's at the top of the ramp, Ava!" Dwight reached back and grabbed Ava's shoulder.

Camellia stood up and saw that Dwight was right. Something long and dark and thick was stretched out almost the full width of the ramp.

"I can't turn now," Ava glanced over her shoulder. "I might really hurt him if I slowed down."

"It's a snake!" Camellia clutched her throat, her stomach reeled from the thump of Malcolm's skis hitting the ramp.

Camellia saw him do a little shuffle just as he reached the top of the jump and saw the snake in his path, but Malcolm didn't lose his nerve. Instead, he simply plowed right through the snake, sloppily rolling it along until they reached the end of the ramp when the snake seemed to go off in several different directions and Malcolm lifted into the air, kind of kicking his feet and doing a semi-turn as he came down, still holding to the tow line. As soon as he landed, he dropped the bar and yelled toward the boat.

Ava sagged with relief to see her husband able to wave to them with both hands. "I've never seen a snake on a ski jump before."

"If you think about it, that's a perfect place to sun yourself." Dwight sounded calm once again as he rocked his way to the back of the boat to help Camellia pull Malcolm in. "This ain't your week is it?" He yelled at Malcolm.

Malcolm spit water, wagging his head. "I think the son of a bitch bit me. I felt a sting in my leg, and it hurts like hell."

Dwight leaned over, grabbed the lower half of Malcolm's vest and lifted him in one motion into the boat. Camellia slid to the side as Malcolm bumped into the boat, and for a moment, she couldn't comprehend why Malcolm had mud smeared down his right calf. Where would he have picked up a streak of mud in water this deep? But then Camellia realized she wasn't looking at mud. She was looking at the top eight inches of the snake that Malcolm had just skiied through.

"Dwight, it's still got him!" Camellia started smacking at the remains of the snake.

"Damned if it don't!" Dwight reached down and grabbed the snake's head. "Hooked himself in that muscle up to his gums." He slung the snake as far as he could. "No wonder you people like to ski. This is exciting!"

Ava had clambered to the back where Dwight was easing Malcolm to the bench seat. "Don't we have to suck out the poison?"

"No. You don't do that anymore." Dwight stooped down, looking under the seats. "Where's your battery?"

Malcolm looked up from inspecting his snakebite, his eyes round with his injury. "Ava, get me back to the truck." He pushed her toward the front of the boat.

Camellia showed Dwight where the rear seat lifted up to reveal the battery. "What you want with a battery?" She wondered if Malcolm would admit to his adultery before he died. Having to deal with betraying her husband and having to attend a funeral threatened to overwhelm Camellia. For a moment, she considered telling Dwight right then and there, but then this wasn't the time to be easing her conscience.

Rummaging around in the battery compartment, Dwight didn't answer Camellia for a few seconds. Pulling a tangle of red and green cables out of the compartment, he said to Camellia, "We need these jumper cables too."

Clutching his calf with both hands, Malcolm yelled at Ava. "Get this boat moving! I can feel the poison starting to burn."

"Turn around there, Malcolm." Dwight pushed Malcolm back into his seat. "Get that leg up here." He untangled the jumper cables and put one set of clamps on the seat beside Malcolm.

"Dwight you ought to tell us what you're doing." Camellia rubbed Malcolm's back. She could feel the places where the ticks had bit him. He didn't notice her touch.

Dwight connected the other end of the jumper cables to the boat's battery. "I'm going to neutralize that snake poison." He came back over to where Malcolm was sitting and kneeled down by his bitten leg. "Not three hours ago, I read that electricity can make snake poison mild as milk . . ."

Malcolm jerked his leg away from Dwight. "You going to shock me?"

Sitting down beside Malcolm, Dwight still held the clamps loosely in his hands. "Now Malcolm, I know this don't seem to make any sense to you, but if you'd read that article, you'd understand. All I can tell you is yes it'll hurt. And I'm supposed to slip the juice to you three times. But the electricity will keep the poison from doing so much damage. Once we get back to the truck, you still have a twenty-mile ride to the doctor's office. Let me do it."

Camellia had never heard Dwight's voice sound so persuasive. If he had talked to her like that, she'd have let him hook her up to the battery. Somehow, he sounded as if shocking Malcolm was something he needed to do as much as Malcolm needed to have it done. Following a few moments of brooding silence, Malcolm shifted on the seat and turned his injured leg back toward Dwight.

"Just grab hold of the side of the boat." Dwight slid closer to Malcolm. "You might want to hold something between your teeth. Just don't jump around."

Dwight waited until Malcolm seemed to have found his grip on the boat. Then he pushed one of the clamps hard against the skin an inch or two beside one of the fang holes. After a moment's pause and another look at Malcolm's face, Dwight pushed the other clamp hard against the skin beside the other fang hole. Malcolm stiffened, clenching his eyes. After a second or two, Dwight touched the second clamp to Malcolm's skin again. Another pause then another dose of electricity. The final treatment lasted longer than the first two, and Malcolm had begun to look solidified and vague, like a cement statue.

"Feel better?" Dwight stood up and disconnected the cables from the battery.

"Go to hell." Malcolm slumped in his seat

"Well, if I didn't do anything else, I got your mind off your bee stings." Dwight sat down beside Camellia.

Later in the evening, when they'd come back from the hospital where Malcolm was going to be kept the night for observation, Dwight went back to the river to get Malcolm's boat. Still feeling unsettled by the accident and the shock treatments, Camellia decided she'd look for Casper.

The first two outbuildings she checked were empty. The third she walked to which was closest to Ava and Malcolm's property, looked empty at first. Camellia strained to see any signs of goat in the upper rafters, but the light was fading. Just as she was getting ready to go back to her house, Camellia heard a soft buzzing from overhead. Looking closer at what she thought was a slender shadow at first, Camellia recognized the leg and cloven hoof of a goat sticking out from a wide beam.

Expecting to find the goat in such a place, Camellia had brought along a coil of rope with several fishing weights tied to one end. She threw the weighted end of the rope over the beam, across the goat, then worked the rope back and forth until she scooted the carcass off the beam. Dryly, the dead goat turned a lazy somersault as it fell. Very little was left except the hide and skeleton.

Yet, in the low light of the rickety building, Camellia saw that something inside the goat was giving off a deep golden glow. The buzzing was louder now as well. She stooped over the goat and saw a cloud of bees fleeing their fallen home. She had never seen them make a hive in a goat. Without any hesitation, she touched her finger to the glow slowly spreading from Casper's ribcage. It was honey, and all she wanted was one taste.

Beside the Still Waters

As soon as Lowell Aubain got off from work, he drove eleven miles in the opposite direction from where he lived, where his wife, Jollette, was already fixing his supper. But she would understand and wait, not letting the twins eat before their daddy got home. Back in the bad times, Jollette never waited supper when Lowell was late because she never knew when he might get home, and when he did get home, he seldom had a stomach fit for hot food.

Satisfyingly ashamed of all the years he spent drinking too much, Lowell felt no impatience with the slow moving traffic all around him. Although the furniture factories along this eight mile stretch of industrial road staggered their quitting time in fifteen minute intervals, still too many people were pushing their way home. For the most part, Lowell saw his own face mirrored in many of the faces around him, those fixed in an expression of exhausted serenity. In other faces, he saw the old Lowell Aubain: mad at the world, scowling in anticipation of enjoying some meanness in the hopes of forgetting how empty life was.

In one form or another, Lowell knew that they had all been doing the same thing for the last eight or ten hours. He had been tailing a tenon machine. His particular machine was about ten feet long and made up of what looked like two sets of tank treads. The width of the tenon machine could be adjusted from ten inches to five feet, depending on whether they were working on table tops or drawer braces. The machine operator and Lowell's boss, Old Morris, could spend more than an hour sometimes adjusting the lathe heads that lined the sides of the treads, trying to get the joints to come out shaped perfectly.

Back in the bad days, Lowell had trouble waiting around while Old Morris tinkered with the lathe heads, giving this head a little tap and that head a backhand crack with the lathe wrench, usually knocking the offending blade so far out of kilter in the other direction that Lowell could always count on another thirty minutes of adjustment each time Old Morris lost his temper. Back then, when Lowell had nothing holy to fill up the empty time, he usually sneaked back to the boiler room and smoked a cigarette or two. More satisfying regret at that memory.

Getting caught smoking anywhere inside the plant automatically cost a man his job. But Lowell had figured out over the last five months that when a man was letting his soul burn away day by day, he didn't worry that much about losing his job.

Jollette had dragged him to that first meeting at the Ram in the Bush Tabernacle. Reverend Crosby Parham had succeeded in scaring Lowell in a way he had never been scared before. He had created eternity for Lowell then showed him what was waiting for him there if he didn't change his ways.

While Lowell stood, at the end of the sermon, debating about whether he was scared enough to walk down the aisle—not a very long one now that Lowell could look back, because the Ram in the Bush Tabernacle was set up in one corner of Reverend Crosby Parham's shoe repair store—Jollette had given

Lowell a push. As soon as he realized that she was trying to get by him so she could walk down the aisle and dedicate her life to righteousness, Lowell felt sucked along behind her, with the twins following behind him.

Five months ago, and Lowell hadn't missed a single service. The flock of the Ram in the Bush Tabernacle had continued to grow, the number of those converted was close to thirty, and all of them were begging to be baptized. Then, after the Sunday night service, Reverend Parham had asked Lowell, appointed Lowell, to go out and find a place where the faithful could be fully submerged and sealed against all the demons of the modern world.

Not many people got commissioned for duty by Reverend Crosby Parham. But either the prolonged warm weather—which was making September feel more like July—or the success of the Tabernacle's message was bringing in more shoe repairs than the Reverend could ever remember. Jollette had told Lowell as they drove home from the meeting that being asked to find a baptizing pool was almost as good as being appointed a deacon. Flattered as he felt by his wife's admiration, Lowell tried to fight down the slick sin of pride. Still, he had to admit if anybody knew the rivers and creeks of Hibriten County, N.C., it was Lowell Aubain.

The fumes from the cars around Lowell brought to his mind all those nights he had spent on riverbanks, burning a tire to keep the mosquitoes away, watching his fishing line with one eye and his liquor line with the other. Nibbling at the devil's bait with more appetite than any fish he'd ever pulled out of the water.

Not that fishing was a sin. Lowell took a quick look around. He'd never thought that fishing was a sin. Practically all the disciples had fished. Although Lowell had some questions about the manliness of using a net. This was a doubt he figured he'd never be reckless enough to voice. Deep down, he suspected that the fishermen's wives had talked them into using a net instead of going after the fish one-on-one. Wives always wanted their men to trade adventure for business. Another warning flash from Lowell's conscience.

No, wives just wanted what was best for their families. Reverend Crosby Parham always made a point of mentioning how important it was for women to be wives. It completed the woman and corrected her man. Lowell nodded, relieved to be back on firm mental ground once again. To rest his eyes from the glare off the rear bumper of the sluggish car in front of him, Lowell contemplated the rows and rows of cars still parked in the lots on either side of the road. In ten minutes, those cars would be filled with men and women intent on worming their way into the traffic. Behind the parking lots rose the massive factories, flanked here and there by their lumberyards, the sweet smell of raw pine wood riding the dusty air almost like a promise of rain, a hope of relief.

When Jollette had suggested, after he'd been saved, that Lowell needed to give up fishing as well as the drinking, he'd felt a deep swoop in the walls of his stomach. He'd loved being out under the stars, standing on a sandy bank, listening to water dodge around the rocks and roots around his feet.

"What you love is being away from your family." Jollette hadn't exactly accused him when she argued this point, but she swung her eyes like a bat up against the side of his head.

"What you love is the darkness." Reverend Crosby Parham squeezed Lowell's arm when he warned him about the dangers of night fishing.

In the split second Lowell had taken these words, his wife's and his pastor's, and linked them together, he fell down on his knees between Jollette and Reverend Crosby Parham and almost gagged on his guilt. They had both snagged him, conviction lodged down in his gut like a steel Eagle Claw hook. He had gone to the river some nights the way he sometimes went into his and Jollette's bedroom, when he knew she had been in the sexy department at K-Mart and she had bought something that was slick under his fingers and moved under his caress like a shallow puddle of warm water.

After five months of deliberately staying away from the water, Lowell knew he had to be careful. Knifing through the stubborn odors accumulated inside his car–the years of sweat, of spilled drinks and dropped food, of leaking fuel lines and overheated oil, of the twins' vomit and tipped over bait buckets–the fishy, mossy, piney scent of the river stirred some of the old dark blood that Lowell was still trying to pray out of his system. The river smell promised privacy, even intimacy with a touch of risk.

He parked his car in the rutted lot behind the old pump plant, a square, two-story building with dark blue glass in the windows which had housed as far back as Lowell could re-member a deep hum which attached itself to people's molars and body hair. Even fully clothed and worn out from a day's work, Lowell immediately felt the hairs on his legs beginning to vibrate.

The road, never kept in very good repair, sloped on down past the pump house, widened about fifteen feet before it reached the water, then gave itself up to the green water of the Catawba River. This was a boat ramp, but a treacherous one because it wasn't maintained. About ten feet out, the gravel and cement just crumbled away to red clay. If a boater didn't know what he was doing, he was likely to find himself launching his trailer along with his boat.

Lowell and his buddies used to come out here when they were younger and sinful just to watch people lose their trailers and sometimes their cars. The ramp was hardly used at all these days, and swimmers didn't like the little beach because the hum from the pump plant couldn't be ignored for too long. It made people want to go home and bathe or make love. Many years ago, however, Lowell had discovered that if you could get drunk enough the hum got easier to endure.

The scenery at this part of the river was certainly all that a baptizing service could want. Pine trees, mingled with a few hardwoods, held their limbs right out over the water as if giving a blessing. Across the broad river, a dense forest, mounted on a series of gentle but high hills, tinted the smooth water an even deeper green.

Leaning slightly back against the slope of the ramp, Lowell eased his toes to the very edge of the water, studying the depth. Reverend Crosby Parham could wade out about seven feet. That'd put him up to his waist and he'd still not be in danger of getting on the slippery end of the ramp. Add the thirty people who planned to get baptized who'd probably bring at least two family members and then the forty other members of the congregation who hadn't felt the need to get baptized—yet—and the friends and family they'd bring along, Lowell figured the small beach would just about hold all of them.

The folks getting baptized could line up easily enough on the ramp. Lowell glanced up the ramp and nodded. They'd decided to wear robes to get baptized in. White robes. In the bad days, he'd relished the white bathing suits that some women wore. When the suits got wet . . .

Lowell jumped back from the water. He saw that the toes of his shoes had gotten wet. Some blonde in a motorboat had worn a white bathing suit. She'd been skiing and the pink of her skin had been visible through the soaked fabric not to mention all the other colors . . .

But as a man commissioned to find a baptismal pool, Lowell knew he had no business letting himself remember that woman. What he needed to do was focus on the joy of that baptismal service, all of them in their white robes. He made himself think of Jollette rising up out of the water . . . but then he couldn't help but see the wet robe clinging. Backing even further from the edge of the water, Lowell commanded himself to ask Jollette just exactly what she planned to wear under her robe.

Before he could get turned completely around and headed up the road by the pump house, Lowell realized that he was tingling, up his arms and legs—all the way up his legs to where he stopped having legs and the tingling didn't stop even there. Then he knew this was the hum. And he knew this place couldn't ever be graced with a baptismal service. Not without a lot of drinking before they got into their soon-to-be-wet robes.

Clenching his teeth until his ears locked up, humming "When the Roll Is Called Up Yonder" through his nose until he smelled the capillaries swollen with blood, Lowell sped out of the parking lot of the pump house, rolling up his window despite the heat, hoping to sweat his body back into piety, into the peace he saw as his salvation. This part of the river was too close, too private. It was maybe a gate to hell for all Lowell knew. All those trees closing in around the water. And that hum. Those trees just kept that hum right there up against a person.

Maybe a baptismal pool needed to be more open, more exposed to the sky, to the blue floor of heaven. Less dark places to let the wrong thoughts grow. As Lowell turned his car toward another beach he knew of, his heart grew calm once again. He had struggled against the river and won. He wondered if maybe Reverend Crosby Parham had given him this task as a test. Then briefly, the old mean Lowell asked, as reasonably as he could, "Why ain't he testing everybody else?"

But it was an honor to be tested. Lowell nodded to himself. Just maybe he had more to prove. Nobody else in the Ram in the Bush Tabernacle had given over so completely to drink and night fishing as Lowell had. Pleasure had been the trap. The first three or four swigs of everclear brought the stars into firmer focus. Then he could sit on a log, pour himself some coffee out of the thermos jug and feel about as broad and soft as one of his mama's quilts. He knew the liquor had done its first duty by him when he had to rub his arms and legs to assure himself that he still had clothes on.

If he got a strike before he took his next set of drinks, usually three or four deep swigs of everclear, he either ignored it or jerked the rod around just enough to lose the fish. To really enjoy fishing, Lowell had to feel like the river. And he suspected that nobody could feel like the river in broad daylight. You couldn't see the edge of your skin or the ends of your fingers and know what the river felt like. There had to be some confusion, some melting, some unraveling.

As soon as Lowell topped the hill that rose up above the Rhodhiss Dam, he could see down below him the wide open expanse that had once been Rhodhiss Beach. On the far side of the river, the trees had been severely thinned out by a lumber company. On the side of the river where Lowell eased his car into a heavily eroded parking lot, the pine trees were kept well under control by the rocks and sand that had once made Rhodhiss Beach the busiest summer attraction in this end of Hibriten County.

Even the river odor here was thinned out, maybe evaporated more easily because the sun baked the landscape all day long. If a person wanted shade at Rhodhiss Beach, he'd better bring it along with him. At least, that was the rule when people used to come to the beach. When Lowell had been a teenager, all of the people who worked in the Rhodhiss cotton mills—especially the people who worked the graveyard shift—spent their days on Rhodhiss Beach. With the closing of the mills, the beach got emptier and emptier.

It was quiet here. No hum. Lowell walked down toward the water. The sand wasn't as deep as it used to be; the red clay natural to the river's banks was beginning to push through along the beach. In some places, clumps of limbs, warped cardboard, and fragmented Styrofoam festooned with shredded plastic and disemboweled cassette tapes seemed more permanently planted than the pale sand. Lowell wondered if he could get some volunteers from the Tabernacle to help him clean up the beach before the baptizing.

The slope of the beach once it entered the water looked pretty easy to Lowell. He squatted down at the edge of the water. Rhodhiss Beach had always been friendly. Friendly water, friendly sand. Friendly people. The mill people especially. A lot of them came out to the beach just so they could sleep, those who had been working up until seven o'clock that morning. And when they did roll over out of their naps and push themselves up on their elbows to check and see if their kids had drowned, they would talk to you in sleepy voices that felt like the thick warm water.

Back then, Rhodhiss Beach had a wooden raft about thirty yards from the shore. Lowell remembered swimming, as best he could, out to that raft and stretching out on its smooth planks, positioning himself so he could rest his chin on his forearms and study all the people sunbathing and sleeping on the beach. There was always two or three women who had a way of turning their stomachs up to the sun, giving themselves up to anybody who wanted to stare at them . . .

Lowell stood up so quickly that he had to fight off a dizzy spell. He cocked his head toward the dam just to make sure that some piece of machinery over that way wasn't sneaking in a hum on him. No. The quiet in this place was just about reverent. With plenty of places for friends and family to sit, although they'd probably need to wear hats or carry umbrellas to keep the sun off of them.

What with the trees on the far side of the river all cut down and trees on this side of the river pushed back out of the way, Lowell felt totally exposed. And that was the way a religous man should feel, wasn't it. Open to anyone's curiosity and inspection. Yes, he remembered the thoughts he'd had as a young man when girls came down to the sand, spread out their blankets, rubbed oil on themselves, then gave themselves up to the sun and the eyes of anybody who was interested, their finest curves glittering with their oil and the sweat that would smell like coconut and pineapple and then finally like a woman . . .

Unable to get all the traction his soul demanded as he scrambled over the sand and clay beach, Lowell came close to dropping to all fours in order to get away from the seductive water. When he finally reached the higher ground of weeds and gravel that seemed more a part of the parking lot than the beach, Lowell paused to catch his breath and study the river. Had he actually, only five months ago, made regular trips to such places as this at night when he was not even half sober?

Had the river in the darkness pulled him to these same vain cravings? Well, he and his buddies had talked about women and sex on some fishing trips. And he had wondered about some of the women he saw in the factory. His quick review of what thoughts he could remember from his years as a night fisherman confirmed for Lowell that he had been possessed by a sexual demon that lived in the river–that river right there in front of him. It swam right up to him even when he stood by the water in the daylight. All Lowell could do was move his search to a different stream.

Not wanting to go home before he found a baptismal pool, Lowell thought maybe he should look somewhere far away from the Catawba River. Too many places along that stretch of water had a hold of Lowell in all the wrong places. Sometime down the track, Lowell wanted to ask Reverend Parham just why sex had to be connected to parenthood. It made no sense to Lowell. Children shouldn't come from a man and a woman getting together in a dark room. Especially two children at the same time.

Lowell hunched his shoulders and shook his head at himself. Oh, he loved his two boys all right. But when he saw the two of them in the hospital nursery, he felt afraid. His buddies at work had kidded him about letting Jollette have it with both barrels, but in the seven years since the twins had been born, Lowell had tried to be very careful with Jollette. She could still get him steamed up, get him wanting her like a bull wanting a bellow, but no matter how long he waited from one time till the next, at the end, when he knew he couldn't hold back any longer, he always felt afraid. He didn't know what he'd do with another set of twins, and although the Ram in the Bush Tabernacle didn't have any specific rules against birth control, Reverend Parham had made his views clear on the subject of sex without the intent to have children.

Maybe after his baptism, Lowell would not be tormented by the sexual demon. He wondered if when he was drunk the demon was less interested in him. Of course, that antidote wouldn't help him much at the baptizing services . . . unless he could sneak in a few drinks before actually going.

No. Breaking out into a mild sweat, Lowell reminded himself that if he could just find a pool or a pond that wasn't possessed, then he could go into the water without being tempted to stare at the places where the women's robes clung to their bodies. All he had to do was find water that was innocent. To do that, Lowell realized, all he had to do was go back to a place he used to play when he was a small child, when all he cared about was the water itself and not the effects it had on the flesh of women.

Gunpowder Creek. It was the only body of water Lowell could remember exploring when he was too young to be interested in girls. And the swimming hole he remembered wasn't that hard to get to.

Just across the one-lane bridge which spanned the creek, Lowell was happy to see that the road had two wide shoulders. In fact, on the side of the road where he parked, an old logging road headed down toward the swimming hole. There'd be plenty of room to park. But he knew the logging road fell apart about seventy yards into the woods. Still, the path was easy enough to follow after the road gave out. The local kids still probably used the place. Here and there along the path, Lowell was surprised to discover antique piles of trash, identical to the piles that he had seen twenty years ago as he and his friends made their way down to the swimming hole. Some of the discarded appliances, Lowell would almost swear, were the same ones which were nearly rusted away all those years ago.

The path took a sharp turn to the right and ended at the lip of a sandy slope which dropped down to the gray water of Gunpowder Creek, just as Lowell remembered. With a flutter similar to the thrill of salvation, Lowell recognized his childhood playground. Even twenty years later, he couldn't believe his luck to have found such a perfect swimming hole—now a perfect baptismal pool.

For most of its length, Gunpowder Creek was adequate mainly as a wading creek. On the average, it was ten or fifteen feet wide and knee deep. But the swimming hole, through some twist of geology, was close to thirty feet wide for a stretch of ninety feet, and in some places, it was close to four feet deep. The small beach could certainly accommodate all the candidates for baptism while the spectators could stand up on the rim of the shore, stretched out along the path in double file. Lowell nodded as he did these visual calculations. Plenty of room. Kind of like an auditorium.

And the woods didn't present a problem. Although they were thick enough to give the congregation privacy, enough big trees had been cut, and cut again, that nobody needed to worry about his dirty thoughts being able to find shelter. Cautiously, Lowell walked through the sand toward the water. He let his moral grip on his mind loosen. No hum threatened him. No big open smooth stretches of water like women posing half naked on their towels. Lowell let himself think about those women for a moment. His body didn't respond by trying to shove its way next to the women. It was innocent water.

Lowell moved closer to the creek's edge. He'd have to do some picking up. In the shallow water upstream sat half a suitcase. Along the bank, a large car radiator tilted against a ragged tree stump, slimy grass dripping down into the water from the grillwork. Not five feet from where Lowell stood, a white-wall Roadhandler tire, half buried in mud, gaped up at the sky.

Cleaning up the place wouldn't take long. Lowell figured he could just move the trash further on down the path out of sight, but when he bent down to jerk the tire out of the mud, he noticed a large brown lump wedged against an exposed root on the far side of the bank.

A person was Lowell's first thought. Looked too rectangular to be a person, though. Too big to be a dog. As he studied the lump, Lowell realized he was looking at fur. But there was too much of it to be a dog, unless it was an awfully big dog, a dog bigger than Lowell had ever seen. Could be a person in a fur coat. If that was the case, Lowell figured he was obligated to pull the body out of the water.

Sitting down on a fallen tree trunk, Lowell pulled off his shoes and socks. He was going to get wet, probably up past his belly. Did he want to take off his pants and be almost naked in the water with maybe a dead woman in a fur coat. Lowell was pretty sure the lump was a woman because no man he knew would wear a fur coat. Since he'd just get his clothes wet anyway when he put them back on, Lowell decided to wade over fully dressed, except for his shoes. Then again, he didn't know what might be on the bottom of the creek, so he put his socks and shoes back on. He felt better this way.

The banks of the creek were steeper than he remembered and after three stumbling steps, Lowell was already up to his knees. By the time he reached the middle of the creek, the water was up to his waist. He had to keep his attention focused so much on his footing that Lowell didn't recognize the lump as a deer carcass until he was right beside it.

On this side of the creek, the water was up to Lowell's shoulders, and he was having trouble keeping his balance. He didn't intend to touch the carcass as hard as he did. Clearly the deer had been dead and afloat for a long time. It was bloated and thumped like cardboard when Lowell, floundering, bumped his hand against its side.

Pulling the body from against the root where it was snagged, Lowell hoped he didn't shove an antler into his side. But as soon as the deer came free and drifted around, Lowell knew he didn't have to worry about antlers. The head had been cut off. Raggedly and in a hurry from what Lowell could tell. Well, what would you expect from somebody who'd collect deer trophies out of season. Maybe they ran over it and decided not to waste a good rack. Just cut off its head and toss the rest in the creek. A stench rose from what seemed like the bowels of the dead animal and puffed up through the mushy flesh of the neck.

Lowell twisted his head away from the stink and took a step back, pulling the deer. Keeping his head turned, he reached across the bloated body, trying to get a firmer hold. His fingers sank into a texture that reminded Lowell of overcooked macaroni and cheese. He fought the instinct to jerk his hand away. He had a good grip on the stinking thing—he didn't want to chase it down the creek where he'd just have to grab it again.

When Lowell got to the shallow water, he rolled the deer over so he could use its front legs as handles to pull it up on the bank. As soon as he flipped the carcass over, he discovered that the side he couldn't see felt the way it did because it was completely covered in maggots, pure and white and pulsing. Lowell's forearm was smeared with maggots. Looking across the creek, he saw that he had left a trail of white pellets.

After he had splashed a few yards upstream, Lowell stooped and used the rocky sand from the creek bed to wash the maggots off his arms. He scrubbed until the skin was raw. Stooped over, he studied the deer. Every internal organ in his body had shriveled down to the size of raisins and peach pits. Lowell had his vision of sin, now, clearer than anything Reverend Parham had shared with him.

For the moment, Lowell didn't have a single lust. He was pure. He was thankful. But still, he thought it would be a good idea not to tell anybody what he had pulled from their baptismal pool this day.

Wonderland by Night

Nan Lingle had two reasons for weedeating around her house immediately before lunch even though she ran the risk of heatstroke and nausea: by that time of day, the grass that grew against the side of her house wasn't so sticky, and that was the time when she was least likely to witness the spectacle of her neighbor, Amaryllis Widdicomb, sporting all over her shady yard with her live-in boyfriend, Wyatt Tramble. Although Nan had been married for thirty-two years and had two grown daughters, she still couldn't reliably distinguish between Amaryllis's and Wyatt's fights and their foreplay.

When the two of them drank, they got vaguely threatening. In the last month, Nan had seen Wyatt chasing Amaryllis around their yard five different times, him in a pair of camouflage underwear and her in a beach towel advertising Morehead City. Neither one of them spoke during their chases. They uttered sounds—gasps, grunts, maybe some sobs. Nor could Nan decipher their mood or intentions from how they ran. Usually drunk, always barefoot, and Amaryllis's yard, thick with black walnut trees, stayed covered with the lumpy, sour smelling nuts, so in their pursuit of each other, Amaryllis and Wyatt slid and wobbled a great deal.

Since Amaryllis had moved in three months ago and started her frolics in the yard, Nan had waited for the other neighbors to complain, to register some mark of concern for what was happening to the neighborhood. Shamefully, all of them had a reason for not calling the police. Over the past two years, the town of Hibriten had been doing such a good job of making Nan's neighborhood a showplace that she and her neighbors secretly worried that if they complained too much about each other, the civic improvements might go to another part of town.

Besides, the real troublemakers up at the far end of the neighborhood had been scattered by the machinery of civic improvement. All of the old textile mill houses at the top of the hill had been torn down. All of the mill workers had to relocate themselves, finally go out and buy or rent their own houses instead of leeching off their employer, practically living rent free until the mill went bankrupt.

Then they'd torn down the ancient barbed wire fence around the cow pasture just across from Nan and Gordon's house and built a pedestrian park. She and Gordon tried to do the three-mile loop every day. On some of the warmer summer evenings, they'd wait until dark to take their walk. Gordon carried a small pistol in a camera case slung from his shoulder. Nan carried a heavy flashlight but didn't have to turn it on because the three-mile loop had peach-colored lamps lighting the path the whole way. Nervous as their night walks made Nan and Gordon, they and their neighbors had agreed that the best way to insure against an influx of thugs was to lay daily and nightly claim to their pedestrian park. Every stroll served as a patrol.

Even over the growl of her Troy-Bilt weedeater, Nan could hear Amaryllis and Wyatt inside their house. Their day was just beginning. Amaryllis had worked for SpunFibers Corporation nearly ten years before that mill went out of business. The graveyard shift. Now she was a night custodian over at the community college. She'd met Wyatt in the community college when he and his crew came in to paint the auditorium. Because the community college taught classes in the auditorium during the day, it had to be painted at night.

All this information Amaryllis offered freely the first day that Nan dropped over on her new neighbor to present her with a bowl of chicken salad—a bowl she hadn't seen since—and to invite her to her church, The Ram in the Thicket Tabernacle. Amaryllis, who had started eating the chicken salad out of the bowl with her finger, paused with one finger hooked over her lower teeth and considered Nan's invitation for several seconds. Then she started laughing so raucously that Nan thought she might split an air passage.

"I don't mean to offend you, Mrs. Lingle." Amaryllis shook her head and gullied her finger through the chicken salad. "But I can't see me and Wyatt spending time in church."

"Oh, now try to peep into this invitation just a little harder." Nan cradled her abdomen on her forearms and rocked back slightly on her heels. On a good day, she invited perhaps thirty people to her church. On any given day, she might have to defend her invitation fifteen or twenty times. "We're a friendly congregation. Not too big." Noticing that Amaryllis wore a faded tube top and cut off blue jeans, Nan suspected that the younger woman belonged to the cult of the comfortable and probably feared a church visit would cripple her forever with modesty. "Real informal. Not like some of them churches where you have to get *all* dressed up."

Amaryllis nodded, sucked her finger, and shifted the bowl of chicken salad to her hip. "Sounds good. Let me think about it." She ran her fingers through her thick hair. "Let me get my life settled down a little, and I'll see."

Then Wyatt had started chasing Amaryllis around the yard, and Nan had seen no signs of Amaryllis's life settling down.

Edging along the outside wall of her and Gordon's bedroom, Nan had to move closer to where her yard joined Amaryllis's. When she eased up on her weedeater's gas trigger, she could just about make out the words bumping between Amaryllis and Wyatt. They were fighting about breakfast. She was telling him if he stayed in her house and didn't work full time, he needed to at least get up and fix their breakfast. Wyatt argued that if Amaryllis hadn't gotten unemployment and severance pay when the textile plant shut down, she couldn't have afforded her house, so she couldn't rightfully claim that she'd worked for the house. In fact, just the opposite was true. She'd got the house because she stopped working. So as far as Wyatt was concerned, she was more obligated to wait on him because nobody had ever given him anything. The least she could do was cook him an egg when he got up.

A fight was brewing. Nan could hear its bitter fluid percolating between Amaryllis and Wyatt like a beverage distilled from those nights lived in a rented house in a textile neighborhood. So far this morning, their argument hadn't moved into the scooting around the kitchen table phase. They'd chase each other around the table for a good thirty minutes. Then they'd get into what sounded like a shoving match in the kitchen. That'd be another fifteen minutes. For another hour or two, they'd drift through the house, and finally, they'd appear on the porch, ready to translate their differences into a game of what Gordon called "open yard grab ass."

Making the turn that brought her along the front of her house, Nan began moving away from Amaryllis's open door. As far as Nan knew, the girl never closed a window or a door once the weather warmed up. She wondered if her two neighbors would be chasing each other when the temperature dropped into the 40's or the 30's. Surely, they wouldn't enjoy themselves so much if they had to put on their coats and gloves. On the other hand, they didn't look like people who owned coats and gloves.

As Nan trimmed around to her side porch and saw that Gordon was pulling the car into their shed, she admitted to herself that she would never be able to see what held some lives together. How could a woman who owned her own house tolerate the graceless existence that Amaryllis woke up to every day? A life so loose she couldn't count on getting an egg cooked with two people sharing the kitchen.

With absolute certainty, Nan knew that she could switch off her weedeater, set it down on the porch right in front of the top step, and before he came into the house for lunch, Gordon would carry that piece of equipment across the yard to their utility shed/garage, and hang it up where it belonged. That was all Nan wanted out of the world of people—neighbors and husbands: just do what they were supposed to do. How could anybody capable of finding her way to work not see that's all that decency amounted to, just doing what you were supposed to do?

As Gordon and Nan ate their late lunch, they could hear the rising voices of their neighbors across their adjacent yards. At this distance, the words were indistinct, but a rhythm had begun to form. It was like a young horse learning how to gallop. For a few minutes, Amaryllis's voice would come out in a sort of roll. Then Wyatt's voice would drop down in a thump. After a few minutes, they'd trade parts. Back and forth, gathering speed.

"How is it they've not killed each other yet?" Nan spooned more potato salad and baked beans onto Gordon's plate. When he'd left for work this morning–his half day of Saturday over-time—he had talked about going fishing after he got home. But if the neighbors were going to fight, Nan wanted her hus-band at home. If she could get him full enough, Gordon would wind up taking a nap instead of going fishing.

"They're just having too much fun going at it." Gordon slid another slice of ham onto his plate. "As long as they're breathing hard, they're satisfied."

"I'm just beginning to think we've been wrong not to call the law on them." Nan had the feeling that Amaryllis and Wyatt were reaching their full speed gallop a lot sooner than usual.

"Wouldn't make much difference." Gordon adjusted his torso, twisting his hips and swaying his ribcage. "All they can do is warn 'em about disturbing the peace. The police'd prob-ably be more irritated with us for calling them than with Am-aryllis and Wyatt. The peace that the law really don't want disturbed is their own. The rest of us just need to get along."

After lunch, Gordon went into the den and turned on a baseball game. Soon, he was asleep. Nan turned up the sound on the television so the neighbors wouldn't disturb her husband; then she went into her bedroom. It sounded as if Amaryllis and Wyatt had moved outside. He was stalking her from tree to tree. The going was slow because the ground rolled with black walnuts in their round sharp-scented husks. The smell made Nan think of what a hospital built by Tarzan might smell like.

Amaryllis never acted like she was afraid of Wyatt, but she always seemed serious about keeping a couple of tree trunks between her and him. Both of them clung to the bark like they were part lizard.

Nan tried to convince herself that if Amaryllis and Wyatt were five or six, this game would be cute, but she knew she wasn't being honest with herself. All too often, when Amaryllis made a move that almost got her caught, she'd throw herself back or scramble out of Wyatt's reach with such desperation that she had to be losing skin off her palms, elbows, and knees. Those times, she'd make noises that blocked the deeper channels of Nan's breathing. They'd tempt Nan to get down on her knees and pray for Amaryllis, but she didn't know exactly what God needed to do in that situation.

In the late afternoon, a heavy shower interrupted Amaryllis and Wyatt. For a few minutes, Nan thought they'd keep after each other in the rain. It had been a long time since Nan had seen such wet skin. Somehow, rain got deeper into people than other kinds of water. Amaryllis's beach towel robe was just a patch of modesty draped from her shoulders. Wyatt's camouflage shorts sucked up against his thighs like original sin. Their skin glistened and tightened against their bones until they looked like they'd been dieting on quicksilver.

II

Because Gordon's nap lasted almost till supper time and they didn't get to take their evening walk because of the storm, he woke up when Nan started groaning in her sleep around 1 o'clock in the morning. She'd first started her nocturnal lamentations about the time their last daughter got married and moved out. He had tried to be an understanding husband, but it was hard on a working man to be kept awake most of the night then have to go trim veneer for eight or ten hours a day. Finally, Gordon asked his doctor what medical science could do for a woman who mourned in her sleep.

The doctor held two definite opinions about Nan's troubled slumber. First, she had clearly entered the early stages of menopause at about the same time her children had left the nest. Second, she needed to lose weight. Naturally, she had to be feeling serious melancholy—most likely amplified by excessive body heat when she lay in bed. According to the doctor, uncontrolled body heat was the leading cause of nightmares and slumber panic. He advised Gordon to do whatever he could to help Nan reduce her body heat at night.

Unsettling as the move felt to Gordon, he and Nan abandoned their old bedroom that was next to their kitchen and bathroom and after thirty-two years of sleeping in the same bed, took up sleeping quarters in the bedroom and the twin beds at the way back of their house, the bedroom Gordon had built for their two daughters when they became teenagers. Somewhat surprising to Gordon, he took only two nights to adjust to the new sleeping arrangements. Although during the first couple of months Nan complained about missing him at night, she did stop groaning.

Shortly after their new neighbors moved down from the mill village, Nan had showed signs of returning to her troubled sleep. This time, Gordon was pretty sure that they couldn't accuse Nan's body heat for the problem. Just as their empty house had depressed Nan a few years ago, the wildness in the house next door was disturbing her now. For Nan, people like their neighbors were more than a nuisance. They were a threat. And when Nan felt threatened, the vibrations reached all the way down into her personal and family history.

When Nan groaned more loudly than usual and pulled herself out of bed, Gordon didn't speak. He knew his wife was going to the bathroom. As he listened to her scuff out of the room, he strained to detect what might have woke her.

Sometimes, the neighbors' arguments got loud enough to seep into Nan's sleep. Gordon thought of the sump pump in his basement. That's what the world needed, more sump pumps in people's lives, something to suck out all the excess drainage.

This was the kind of thought that usually soothed Gordon back to sleep, but just as he started going slack, Nan came back into their bedroom and flipped on the light—something she'd never have done under ordinary circumstances. Gordon sat up, already vaguely alarmed. A light coming on this late at night carried as much foreboding as the phone ringing. Although not expecting to see Nan's face covered in blood, he was barely shocked by the sight. This was exactly the kind of event that would cause Nan to turn on a light at 1 in the morning.

"Lord God!" Gordon jumped out of bed and hurried to grab Nan's elbow. "What happened to your face?"

For a moment, Nan wouldn't let go of the door jamb. "I woke up with an awful headache. When I went to the bathroom to get some Tylenol, I turned on the light and there was all this blood."

Gordon pulled her away from the side of the door and guided her to the bed. "Can you sit here while I go call the ambulance?"

Sitting beside Nan on her bed, waiting for the ambulance, and watching for signs of serious blood loss, Gordon tried to deduce what had caused her injury. His first theory had been that her eyeballs had exploded, but except for some burning when she kept her eyes open too long, she assured him that she could see well enough. Then Nan realized that very soon strange people would be coming into her house and she was sitting there in her pajamas—not even her best pajamas. But when she tried to stand up to change clothes, Gordon clamped his hands on her shoulders and warned her that she might have brain damage and moving around could cause worse problems.

As he kept a tight hold on Nan, Gordon checked the ceiling over her bed. He'd been as careful as he knew how when he installed the dry wall for the ceiling, but maybe he'd cracked a sheet during installation and it had been working itself loose for the last ten years, finally to fall on his wife's head. Or maybe the heavy rain had leaked through the roof and weakened part of the ceiling.

Nope. Not a sign of ceiling failure. Neither of the two windows in the room was broken. For a moment, Gordon took his hands from Nan's shoulders and leaned over to check for a wild animal under her bed. Gordon had heard of land developments displacing animal populations, forcing them to move in closer to their human neighbors. The woods that had been cut down to make the pedestrian park could have held dozens of raccoons, opossums, and woodchucks. Not to mention squirrels, snakes, foxes, and even a bobcat or two. But underneath the bed was as blameless as the ceiling. Nothing crouched in the shadow of Nan's box springs.

Taking his wife's hand in both of his, Gordon leaned against her arm. "You didn't go to bed with a pair of scissors or a knife, did you?"

"Don't get foolish with me, Gordon." Nan touched her chin with an index finger and tapped it along her jaw then into the hollows of her cheeks. The blood there seemed to be drying. "Ought we to wash some of this mess off?"

"We don't touch anything." Gordon pushed her free hand down into her lap. "The ambulance people need to see how much blood you've lost." He studied her face, leaning across her lap to get a better view of the far side of her head. "We don't know where you're bleeding from."

"Do you think God might have struck me?" Nan squeezed Gordon's hand and blinked heavily through the congealing blood.

If they had been sitting in a tent in ancient Israel, Gordon could have conceded that Nan's fearful explanation might have some foundation for concern. But sitting in their bedroom with a hundred watt bulb civilizing the night and the pink streetlamps across the street enchanting the pedestrian park, Gordon wanted to believe that God had changed His way of warning people about their secret sins. Besides, what transgression could his wife harbor that might move God to bloody her head? If God started handing out head injuries as the wages of sin, how many people would be waking up completely decapitated? Gordon ran the palm of his hand down the front of his face. Why hadn't he rolled out of bed leaking blood from his eyes, ears, and nose?

"In the thirty-two years I've known you, I haven't seen you sin enough to deserve a mosquito bite." He patted Nan's knee.

"I've always thought I needed to witness more. You know, try to carry God's message to more needful souls." Nan clenched her eyes and squeezed out a slow strand of tears. "Like them people next door."

"Don't start crying." Gordon thought about pulling a handkerchief out of his dresser, but he couldn't see himself wiping over what might be raw flesh where his wife's skin used to be. "If you're crying when the ambulance people get here, you're really going to confuse them."

For a moment, Nan doubled over like she was going to put her head between her knees. Then she pulled her back straight again. "Lord, I hope this ain't the start of some awful disease."

"Well, except for the blood, you don't seem that sick to me." Gordon raised the tips of his fingers to the side of Nan's neck. "I don't feel a fever."

"Do I look pale?"

"Now, Nan, pale's the last color anybody could call you." Gordon stood up and stooped closer to his wife's face.

"Do you hurt?"

"I've still got that old headache." Nan tilted her head then lightly touched her hair, her fingers inspecting her scalp. "The top half of my face feels like it's sunburned."

For a few seconds, Gordon's mind involuntarily filled with television images from shows about Hiroshima and Nagasaki. Radiation. Years and years ago, the old volunteer fire department was located beside the now bankrupt SpunFibers loading docks up at the end of their street. Once or twice a month, their neighborhood would be awakened by the fire siren calling the volunteers to the department. Of course, all those signals were sent by radio and telephone now so the siren hadn't blown in close to a decade. Still, Gordon remembered that in the event of a nuclear attack, the fire signal was supposed to serve as the air raid signal. Through most of the 60's and 70's whenever the fire siren woke Gordon up in the middle of the night, he'd lie in bed, half asleep, praying that it was just somebody's house afire and not the end of civilization.

Leaning closer to Nan, he searched for signs of radiation burns. Too much blood to get a clear view of her skin. He couldn't remember if burned skin gave off that much blood. He glanced at the wall beside her pillow. No sign of nuclear attack that he could see, no discolored paint or melted sheetrock. To reassure himself that Hibriten hadn't been leveled by an atomic bomb, he raised himself enough to look out the window over Nan's bed. Wouldn't the shock wave knock out the glass? Outside, the boxwoods lining their sidewalk and their two magnolia trees in the front yard flickered in a breeze left over from the thunderstorm, but nothing was blasted flat or vaporized.

"You think I might have been struck by lightning?" Nan grabbed Gordon's elbow and pulled him back beside her.

"That would be a good explanation." Gordon glanced back at Nan's window then at the window over his bed. Neither one was damaged. "But I don't see anyplace where it might have come in."

"Maybe it came in at a peculiar angle and didn't leave a mark."

"Nan, I've never seen lightning not leave a mark." Gordon wondered if he really knew what he was talking about. Maybe lightning could come through a closed window somehow and not necessarily break it. Maybe those people who died from spontaneous combustion had really been struck by some kind of mutated lightning.

Gordon was both relieved and irritated by the two men who arrived in the ambulance because the first thing they wanted to know when they looked at Nan was how she had received her injury. From the way one of the men glanced over his shoulder at him, Gordon could tell he was a suspect. As soon as Nan began explaining that she had no idea how she'd been injured, even Gordon had to admit their ignorance sounded terribly suspicious.

Both men slipped on latex gloves and turned their full attention to Nan's condition. One took her blood pressure while the other began feeling along her jaw, then her cheeks. When he pressed his fingers over the center of Nan's forehead, she jerked away from him with a noise that Gordon had never heard from her. It sounded like she'd swallowed a rusty bedspring. For all the years that Gordon had listened to Nan, her noises usually came from deeper, softer sources.

"Looks like we've found the damage." The ambulance man examined Nan's forehead more closely. "Hand me a sponge."

When the man had wiped the blood from Nan's forehead, Gordon could see a gash angling from her left eyebrow to the right corner of her hairline. Tears gathered in the corners of Nan's eyes.

"You're sure you don't know how you got this laceration?" The ambulance man looked at Nan, but his voice reached in Gordon's direction.

III

It was still dark when Gordon turned onto their street and drove Nan by the forlorn and antique brick walls of the SpunFibers Textile Plant. Although Nan had been sincerely relieved when the plant closed and the mill houses had been bulldozed to make way for four little league baseball fields, she couldn't help but feel a sense of loss that orbited irregularly through her daily emotions. Especially on gloomy evenings and moonless nights if she happened to catch a glimpse of the abandoned building, she couldn't help but think she was looking at the remnants of a lost civilization. Quite often in Sunday school, Nan could get lost when they started talking about all those tribes scattered by the Israelites. Families drifting apart.

She was grateful for the medication the emergency room doctor had given her. He'd also put ten stitches in her forehead and wouldn't stop questioning her about the mystery of how she'd been injured. And Gordon standing right there beside her the whole time, holding her hand. Eventually, the doctor must have noticed how rattled Nan's injury had left Gordon, and he stopped slinging his suspicions around so freely.

"I bet you feel like you've been through the wringer." Gordon shook his head and yawned.

"I don't think I can make it to church this morning." For a second or two, Nan entertained the idea of making the effort to get cleaned up and dressed for service, but she knew she would be acting out of vanity. She had always been critical of people who used church as a display case for their suffering.

"Part of the deal I made with that doctor was he wouldn't make you spend the night if I'd bring you right home and slap you in the bed." Gordon slowed down and gazed at Nan. "What did happen to you?"

Nan shook her head. Now they were past the baseball fields and entering the pink glow coming from the pedestrian park. A couple of her neighbors had grumbled about the light from the park, but Nan was glad to have the once dark meadow civilized with the gravel paths and illuminated against the night. During the opening ceremonies for the pedestrian park, a song that had played over and over again from the PA speakers was "Wonderland by Night." And now, through the haze of her visit to the emergency room, Nan could see the park absorbing all that peach fuzz light, softening its contours and vibrating with the health it planned to impart to anyone who would faithfully follow its loops.

While Gordon unlocked the front door, he made Nan sit in their porch swing. She had to admit that she was feeling pretty light headed, but just as she heard the lock click open, she also heard the gravel in their driveway crunching under the tires of a Hibriten Police car.

As he helped Nan stand up from the swing, Gordon kept his eyes on the young policeman walking up to their porch. ""I bet you got a call from the emergency room this morning."

Nan was glad it was still dark because she knew neither she nor Gordon was comfortable with being suspects. But Gordon would be mortified. It was one thing to be questioned by a doctor, something else entirely to be questioned by the police.

"Can I talk to you for just a few minutes?" The young policeman removed his hat and clamped it under his elbow. "I know you're tired, but for your own safety, we need to track down how your wife got hurt."

"Son, it's 4:30 in the morning." Gordon pushed open the door, keeping one arm around Nan. "Can't you come back after I've got my wife back in her bed? The medicine the doctor gave her is supposed to knock her legs right out from under her." While Gordon guided Nan into their den with one arm, he held the door open for the policeman with his other arm.

Following Gordon and Nan into their house, the policeman glanced around their den. Nan felt her leg bones wobble slightly, as if she stood knee deep in the ocean with the waves breaking about fifty feet away. Despite the unsteadiness rising through her knees, she felt unexpectedly connected to her den, her husband, and her policeman. Maybe it was the pain killer the doctor had given her. Or maybe her injury was like a new eye to see through. But she understood that the young policeman had come to help them, even though, Nan could also see, he was looking for signs of a struggle, perhaps even a weapon.

"Can't you come back around lunch?" Nan felt her skin beginning to tingle. It was as if her own voice excited her. "I would ask you to come back for breakfast, but I don't think I'll be back to my old self by breakfast."

"I'm sorry, but when we get a report of a dispute leading to injury, we have to investigate as soon as we make contact with the concerned parties." The policeman took his cap from under his elbow, hooked four fingers along the rim, then rested it on his hip.

Nan felt Gordon's arm tighten. She pushed him toward their bedroom. "Why don't you go straighten my bed for me. I'll tell the policeman what happened. What didn't happen." Nan started to laugh, but as soon as the skin along her forehead tightened, she saw bright flashes of light in the corners of her eyes until she had to press her palms along the side of her head to ease the sting of her stitches. "Whatever happened, Gordon slept through it."

Reluctantly, Gordon shuffled a couple of steps toward their bedroom.

Then the policeman said, "Well, I do like to talk to the concerned parties separately." He nodded in Gordon's direction. "This kind of cooperation will speed up my investigation."

Nan eased herself down on the arm of their sofa. She knew she could get Gordon or the policeman to help her up when the time came. "If you want to check on disputes, you need to see the people in the house over there." Nan pointed, but her arm wanted to sway. She watched it for several seconds, wondering if she needed to explain more fully to the policeman which neighbor she meant. Her religion warned her about bearing false witness.

"Just tell me, Mrs. Lingle, did your husband cause that injury on your head?" The policeman stepped closer to Nan. "You don't have to be afraid. Did he hit you? Or push you into a shelf or a door?"

Nan wanted to laugh again, but she took a deep breath and pressed her hands against her head once more to calm her buzzing skin. "You're asking the wrong people." Nan kept her hands on her head but turned to look directly into the policeman's eyes. "All the disputes take place next door."

Before the policeman could ask another question, Gordon bustled through the door. "I started to change your bedclothes, Nan. You got blood all over your sheets and pillow case. But when I started tucking in your new sheet, I slid my hand along the wall, and I thought I felt a little draft." Gordon motioned for the policeman to come with him. "I felt around and found a little round hole about nine inches above your bed, Nan."

The two men disappeared from the den, through the living room, and into the bedroom. Nan squeezed her knees together and pulled herself up, clinging to the door jamb, straining to catch the conversation going on between Gordon and the policeman. She could see first Gordon then the policeman squatting by her bed, poking their fingers into her wall. With one finger still stuck in her wall, the policeman angled his arm then sighted along his shoulder. His cheek still pressed against his shoulder, the policeman gave directions to Gordon who walked toward the wall at the head of his bed and stooped down, rubbing the wall with his three middle fingers.

Nan swayed as she walked, her whole body reminding her of her unsteady arm. But this unsteadiness didn't connect her to weakness. She thought she could walk like this all night. Just drift over to the pedestrian park and loop around the meadow till she felt fully like herself again. It was like being in an April morning fog. Vague but refreshed. Through the slats in their living room blinds, the peach glow from the street-lights brushed her skin like bunny fur.

In the bedroom, both Gordon and the policeman now stooped next to Gordon's bed, their faces hovering close to the wall, their fingers swarming on the wall like bees on the last autumn apple. Neither man noticed her entrance until she lowered herself onto the edge of her bed.

Gordon jumped up and tugged at her elbows. Nan couldn't tell if he was trying to help her up or ease her down.

"We found another hole in that other wall." Gordon kneeled beside Nan. "As far as the policeman can tell, it's a bullet hole that comes in one wall—most likely the wall next to my bed—and goes out through the wall over your bed." Gordon pointed toward his wall then slid his finger through the air toward Nan's wall. "Could you lay down and let us see if your cut matches the angle of the two holes?"

Not wanting to sound disagreeable in front of the policeman, but not wanting to stretch herself out in the company of a strange man—the third to visit her bedroom in the same night—Nan leaned away from Gordon, hoping he would understand her signal, her protest. Instead, Gordon must have thought she was trying to comply with his request, so he pushed her on back until she was staring up at the ceiling.

Sighting across her forehead, Gordon said, "Scoot about two inches to your right."

Then the policeman came and stood over Nan. He kept rocking in and out of her line of vision, making Nan feel even more light headed. "Gordon, why don't you get your ruler and run it from hole to hole?" She knew he kept a 25-foot one in his top dresser drawer with his underwear and handkerchiefs.

Each man took his turn holding the ruler over Nan's forehead. Unexpectedly, Nan wasn't as uncomfortable as she thought she'd be when the young policeman sat down on her bed and gazed along the slightly bowed ribbon of the ruler's blade. At one point, he took her jaw gently between his fingers and tilted her head to the left.

"It's right in line with the holes." Carefully, he lifted the ruler away from Nan's head and smiled. "I think we've got a bullet trajectory crossing through your bedroom."

"That's what I was telling you." Nan propped herself up on her elbows. "We've got a cotton mill worker who lives next door, and she's not been part of the civilized world long enough to . . ."

"Could she have maybe fired a gun toward your house?" The policeman stood up to stare through the window toward their neighbor's house.

"She and her boyfriend are wild enough to have launched a rocket at us if they didn't have to get up too early to press the button." Nan was still trying to grasp the idea of a bullet tearing through their darkened bedroom. She wondered what would have happened if she'd been sleeping on her side. As convoluted as her ear was, she might have woke up with three or four new holes for her earrings.

"I'd better go have a word with them." The policeman paused, tapping his cap against his pocket. "What's the house number over there?"

Because she couldn't force herself to pay attention to Gordon's answer to the policeman's question, Nan realized she must be falling asleep. For fifteen or twenty minutes, she must have been completely passed out, but then she heard Gordon's excited voice saying, "He must've called for another police car. They's three of them over there now."

Before Nan could pull her mind together enough to respond to Gordon, he had bustled out of the bedroom, craning his head over his shoulder, like he wasn't sure if he could find the exact location of the action once he got outside.

In his excitement, Gordon hadn't thought to turn on the bedroom light. Sitting up and planting her feet on the floor, Nan could see her room pulsing in the flashing lights from the three police cars. As she tried to decide if she wanted to witness the policemen breaking down her neighbor's door, Nan leaned slightly to her right and caught sight of a small point of light throbbing halfway up her bedroom wall. It had to be her bullet hole.

She knew she could probably see more easily if she looked out her window, but she didn't want to expose herself. Besides, she needed to see her neighbors getting interrogated through the hole they'd put in her house. Nan stooped down and put her eye to the bullet hole. Because of its angle, Nan had to press her cheek against her wall, but once her vision adjusted, she had a remarkably clear view of her neighbor's porch. On it stood two policemen, Amaryllis, and Wyatt. One policeman dropped a pistol in a paper bag while the other policeman put handcuffs on Wyatt.

The bullet hole not only made the scene appear clearer than real life, but for a few moments, the policemen and Nan's neighbors seemed to move in slow motion. Nan could see the tears on Amaryllis's cheeks as she threw her arms around Wyatt's neck and kissed him like a blind woman. The hole scraped away all of the foolishness surrounding Amaryllis and Wyatt and left visible only their love. For Nan, thinking this was the way God might look at the world, the blue police lights flashing against the peach streetlights magnified Amaryllis's despair. It was the pang of loss and birth. And it caused the kind of gash that a woman had no choice but to forgive.

The Solar-Powered Southern Belle

Sylvia Harper sat on a metal stool to the left of the booth where her daughter, Elaine, was taking her hearing test. The audiologist told Sylvia just before she began the test that children sometimes didn't pay proper attention to the signals if they could see their parents. If Sylvia leaned forward far enough, she could see through the thick glass window of the booth and catch a glimpse of Elaine's head, looking even more fragile than usual, clamped between the bulky earphones the audiologist had talked Elaine into wearing.

As far as Sylvia could remember, this was her first time in a room with an audiologist, a slender red-head in a white lab coat with AUDREY SIMMONS on her name tag. She curved over the control panel in front of her, turning a large knob, keeping her eyes on Elaine, and making small notes on a paper in front of her each time Elaine raised her hand to indicate that she heard the tone. The inside of the booth looked as dull and chilly as a freezer.

A dull tension throbbing in her spine, Sylvia straightened up and let her eyes drift to the wall beside her. Five black frames hung there. All of them contained diplomas or certificates earned by Audrey Simmons. Sylvia took another look at the slim red-head and wondered, as she often did when she met certified women, if they were constantly aware of their accomplishment the way they might be aware of silk underwear. For Sylvia, high school had been a struggle. She had moved to Atlanta for three months of modeling school. But she couldn't adjust to city life. Like the modeling school teachers, city life required her to think of herself and treat herself like a project.

Whenever she sat down in front of a mirror at the modeling school, assigned to apply makeup, Sylvia felt like she was back in sophomore biology about to start her leaf collection or her insect collection. Then there were the walking lessons, the standing lessons, the sitting lessons. All of it had to do with posing. That had been Sylvia's realization nearly nine years ago. Modeling was posing, and it exhausted Sylvia down to her soul. It struck her as such a brittle way to waste time.

Certainly, Sylvia didn't think getting certified was the same thing as posing. Still, she couldn't help but noticing that Audrey Simmons also had a brittle way about her. Perhaps she had a touch of the model in her that had nothing to do with being an audiologist. Or maybe posing was a necessary part of conducting business. And giving a hearing test was business.

The audiologist had stopped turning the knob to give Elaine another set of instructions. She was supposed to raise her left hand if the sound was in her left ear and her right hand if the sound was in her right ear. Sylvia leaned forward to see if Elaine would follow the instructions. She looked very small inside the booth with its egg carton wall paper and its thick door.

Because of her ear infections, Elaine had missed over a month of kindergarten already, and it was just mid-October. The teacher had called Sylvia and suggested that Elaine should be tested for allergies. Although Sylvia had seriously doubted if her daughter had allergies, she had persuaded her husband, Brent, to let her take Elaine to an allergist. Brent had inherited his uncle's truck dealership, but he was skeptical about childhood illness and reluctant to spend money on doctors when no one seemed terribly ill.

To a certain extent, Brent had been proven right when after thirty-four pricks in Elaine's arm and ten injections in her back, she showed no sign that she was allergic to anything—from milk or wheat to cats or dust. When the bill for two hundred dollars had come, Troy brought it into the bathroom where Sylvia was shampooing Elaine's hair and said, "Just let her outgrow it."

Before coming to Elaine's appointment today, Sylvia had stopped by the truck dealership with their daughter. Although she knew that Brent would never object to having Elaine examined, Sylvia had wanted some reassurance that her husband would be willing to follow the doctor's advice—especially if it didn't line up with whatever opinion Brent had formulated over the last couple of weeks as he listened to his daughter and his wife complain about ear problems.

"Well, of course this doctor's going to find something serious wrong with Elaine." Brent propped his elbows on his desk and shook his head over his folded hands. "That's what a specialist does, Sylvia. He's going to charge us special because he's an expert at finding problems where your general doctor doesn't see a thing wrong."

Sylvia had rested one hand against the dark paneling in Brent's office while her other hand plowed through her dark hair. "It is a problem when we have to keep pouring amoxicillin down our daughter's throat to keep her ears from getting infected."

"Why can't you accept that's just the way she is?" Brent leaned back in his chair and spread his arms. "Be happy we can control it with that medicine. Give Elaine time, and she'll outgrow it."

Sylvia straightened her shoulders, ran both hands through her hair, and patted her cheeks. For a moment, she had to concentrate on the front of Brent's maple desk instead of looking at his face. Her mother, Loetha, had not brought her up to argue. Belles did not disagree, Loetha had told her practically every day of her life. Southern Belles charmed, coaxed, appealed to the generosity of the human spirit–but never disagreed. Never confronted. And Brent had been generous, in his own way, to Sylvia's mother after they got married. More than generous if you calculated how much it had cost him to get her out of debt enough to get her electricity turned back on.

Perhaps if the truck business had been brisker, Brent might not be so skeptical of the ear specialist. He never explained, really explained, their finances to Sylvia–except to tell her how low his profit margin was each month. Nevertheless, Brent still managed to get away twice a month for weekend golf games with his buddies. How much money, Sylvia wondered, could Brent be losing if he managed to keep those golf dates?

When she had married Brent, Sylvia had hoped that she could ease up on worrying about money. Such worries had come to her rather late in her life. Often she had speculated that if she had learned to worry about money when she was a child, she might have learned how to deal with her fears of not having enough.

After she had given up on modeling school and come back home, she had realized, for the first time in her life, that everyone she knew was expecting her to do something. By then, her father was spending most of his time away from home, tending to his meat processing business, but when he did stop by for a night or two, he and her mother wanted to know if she was going to look for a job of some sort. Her failure as a model had apparently forced both her parents to reconsider her prospects as a model wife.

Both of them knew that Sylvia wasn't afraid of work. From the time she was old enough to use the household appliances, Sylvia had worked like a maid. She enjoyed cleaning and cooking. Neither of her parents seemed to realize that Sylvia was afraid of applying for a job. On her own, after her failure in Atlanta, Sylvia had gone to stores, intending to ask for application forms, but whether she spoke to the customer service clerk or a cashier, Sylvia always felt squashed by the stare of whoever was in charge of the applications.

Partly what made her nervous was the bad experience she had in high school when she took an office machines course—just as an enrichment course. After two weeks, she still had not come to terms with the photocopier, and the teacher had allowed her to change to library science enrichment because the librarian needed all the people she could get to help her sort and reshelve books. Library work was close enough to housework to allow Sylvia to feel comfortable. In fact, that enrichment course had been her favorite throughout her whole high school career.

In fact, Sylvia had gone to the town library, planning on putting in an application there. She knew that the regular librarians had gone to college, but she thought they might need someone to do the less important jobs. She had gotten very good at shelf reading during her library science course in high school. But as soon as she had approached the front desk at the library and looked into the college educated eyes of the woman checking out books, Sylvia knew it would be harder for her to ask this woman for a job than it would be to ask one of the clerks at the K-Mart for a job.

"Mrs. Harper, if you'll take Elaine over to examination room five, Dr. Childers will see you in a few minutes." Audrey Simmons stood up from her control panel, told Elaine to take off her headset, then motioned for her to go to the door.

"How'd she do?" Sylvia slid off the stool and rubbed her slacks smooth. Except for the occasional party she had to attend with Brent, Sylvia avoided wearing dresses. Since modeling school, she had felt trapped when she wore dresses. And she didn't need to feel anymore trapped than she did before she put her clothes on.

"Fine." Audrey smiled but didn't look directly at Sylvia.

"I thought you conducted the test very well." Sylvia hoped that by being nice to the audiologist, she might get more information than 'fine.'

"Well, Elaine is a pretty smooth operator, herself." Audrey patted Elaine's back.

Leaning closer to the audiologist's ear, Sylvia whispered, "Is her hearing okay?" Then she stooped down to brush Elaine's hair with her fingers. "She's had so many ear infections."

"Dr. Childers is very good about answering whatever questions you might have." Audrey ushered Sylvia and Elaine to the door of the testing room. "He likes to inform his patients about the outcomes of the tests and the examinations just so you'll have the complete picture all at once."

"Well, let's do what we can to make the doctor happy." Sylvia led her daughter through the door and down the hall in the direction that Audrey had pointed. All the examination rooms looked like someone's unheated den—with upholstered wing chairs, rugs, and cherry paneling. But over in one corner of each room stood what looked like a dentist's chair and a small stainless steel sink.

Dr. Childers, like his audiologist, was slim and wore a white lab jacket. He was in his mid-fifties, Sylvia guessed, and doing quite well. His tan announced he was a boat owner, and from his large, sinewy hands, Sylvia would also guess that his boat had sails. She had tried learning how to sail during her first year of marriage to Brent. But she could tell at a glance that Brent would never be the sailor that Dr. Childers was.

After gazing deeply into Elaine's ears and throat, after consulting the audiologist's test results and the x-rays sent by the allergist, Dr. Childers patted Elaine's knee and turned to Sylvia. "Mrs. Harper, Elaine does have enlarged adenoids, just as her allergist diagnosed. And the abnormality isn't allergy related. That's been established." Dr. Childers crossed his legs and scooted his stool closer to Sylvia. "Her eustachian tubes are mildly underdeveloped, smaller at this time than they should be. But we see this condition in children everyday." He smiled and swept his hand around the room. "If I didn't see this condition on a regular basis, I'd be out of business."

Sylvia glanced at Elaine who was frowning and tilting her head toward the door. "Just a minute, Elaine." Sylvia pulled herself to the edge of her chair and rested her elbows on her knees. "Dr. Childers, does all of this mean there's nothing we can do for Elaine's ear infections?"

Dr. Childers' eyes didn't stray the slightest bit from Sylvia's face. Since she was a freshman at high school and the braces had come off her teeth, Sylvia had gotten used to men's gazes. All in one year, her teeth had come out straight and her chest had come out curved. For a few years, she had enjoyed the attention. Modeling school had ruined that pleasure for her. She didn't like thinking about her own attractiveness as packaging. Maybe if she had spent hours getting herself ready to go out and draw men's attention, she wouldn't be so indifferent to it, but on bad days, when she wasn't getting the house cleaned or the clothes washed, she resented the appraisal she had to pass through like an airport metal detector every time she went about her business in the grocery story or the variety store.

"We have three options, Mrs. Harper." Noticing Elaine's growing restlessness, Dr. Childers pulled a shoe box full of stickers from behind the medical chair and handed it to Elaine. "See what you can find in there."

He rolled his chair a few inches closer to Sylvia. "We can let Elaine ride out this infection and hope she outgrows the more chronic problem with her adenoids and her eustachian tubes. Overall, she looks like a healthy child, so I don't see any reason to suspect that her condition won't eventually correct itself." Dr. Childers locked his fingers together on his knee. "Or we could do what your pediatrician's probably already been doing: put her on amoxicillin or Augmentin as a prophylaxis until May." For a few seconds, Dr. Childers studied Sylvia's face.

"That's what we've done for the last two years." Sylvia tried to read Dr. Childers' expression. She thought that both he and his audiologist must take blank lessons from the same expert because she could get no hint of an opinion from his face. For a moment, she didn't like him. What was he hiding? "But Elaine doesn't seem to be making any progress from one year to the next."

Dr. Childers nodded. "Well, our third choice might be the best course of action if you want to see some definite difference in Elaine's health. As you probably already know, Elaine's colds are no worse than any of the other children's that she goes to school with." The doctor shrugged his shoulders and held the shrug as if he expected Sylvia to follow his example.

After two or three seconds, he let his shoulders relax. "Where Elaine runs into trouble is her tendency to get ear infections. She's just not draining enough to keep the fluid from building up. If you ask me, your daughter is a perfect candidate for tubes in her ears. And I'd go ahead and get those adenoids removed too. Enlarged as they are, they certainly contribute to the problem of recurring infection and fluid retention in her ears."

"Tubes?" Sylvia had a vision of the doctor inserting drinking straws deep inside of Elaine's ears. She'd read about this operation in a few magazines, and the allergist had mentioned surgery as a possibility, but not until this moment, hearing "tubes" come out of the doctor's mouth, had she actually thought of them as part of her daughter's head.

Sensitive to the alarm in Sylvia's face and voice, Dr. Childers smiled and reached into his lab pocket. "It's not as bad as it sounds, Mrs. Harper." He pulled out a small plastic case and flipped open the lid. "For a child your daughter's age, the tubes are tiny." Dr. Childers held the case toward Sylvia.

The tubes were about the same size of some of the smallest buttons on one of Elaine's Barbie doll dresses. She studied the tubes for a minute, then placed the case on the doctor's knee. "Does it hurt?"

"The child might feel a little discomfort for a day or two after the surgery, but I've never had a patient who wasn't completely adjusted to them after a month." Dr. Childers put the case back in his pocket then rubbed his knee. For a moment, he seemed to be studying the spot where Sylvia had placed the case.

"Of course, as long as Elaine wore the tubes, you'd have to be very careful about getting water in her ears. But I'd show you how to prevent that in the bath. Usually, I recommend that the child avoid swimming altogether unless you can be sure she won't get her head in the water." Dr. Childers stood up and pushed his stool to one side.

"You think she needs the operation?" Sylvia wanted to stand up too, but she didn't want the doctor to think she was ready to leave just yet.

"Depends on what you mean by 'need.'" Dr. Childers slid his hands into his lab coat pockets. "Without the operation, Elaine isn't in any danger as long as you keep an eye on her ear infections. And you've been doing a good job in that regard. Elaine shows no signs of hearing loss in either ear. But if she does have the operation, I can guarantee that she will have significantly fewer ear infections–if any at all. And the colds that she does have will likely be less intense than what she now experiences."

"You make it sound like the best of all the choices you've given me." Sylvia stood up and moved to the medical chair where Elaine sat, still sorting through the shoe box and attaching stickers to her sweat shirt.

Taking his hands out of his pockets, Dr. Childers moved to the other side of Elaine's chair and let just his fingertips rest on the arm of the chair. "I believe in this procedure. I can remove the adenoids and insert the tubes in about fifteen or twenty minutes. The surgery is done on an outpatient basis. You'd bring Elaine in around six o'clock in the morning. With this operation, I start with the youngest patient and work my way through to the oldest. Elaine would be the second or third person in line–if you decide to go ahead with the procedure. You can wait in the room with her until we take her down to surgery. In less than an hour, she'll be back with you. And if there's no complications, you can be home before noon."

"I'll have to talk it over with my husband." Sylvia stroked Elaine's smooth, dark hair. "The surgery sounds like the way to go as far as I'm concerned. But Brent'll probably have his own set of questions." Keeping her eyes on the top of her daughter's head, Sylvia asked the question she knew Brent would ask her. "How much is this surgery, Dr. Childers?"

"Barring any complications, the tubes, the adenoids, the lab work, and the hospital stay will run right around seventeen hundred dollars, give or take two hundred." Dr. Childers took a step back. "If your husband wants to talk to me, tell him to call here. I'll be glad to answer any of his questions. Most insurance companies cover this procedure. And I do think it's the right treatment for Elaine. It'd be the most comprehensive, in my opinion."

As Sylvia eased her way among the potholes and ruts that used to be her mother's driveway, she wondered how much longer her mother would insist on living in the house her husband was trying so hard to force her out of. Sylvia also wondered how her mother endured the pressure.

Sylvia, Keith, and her mother made a desperate group for about three years, sitting in that big old ranch house that her father, Chester, had designed. Not that big, really, but spacious with eight bedrooms—each with its own private bathroom. And the den with its ten-foot fireplace and the ceiling with the stucco hanging down like stalactites and the dark exposed beams. The whole house had always felt like a cave, and that den looked like something a caveman would live in. For as far back as she could remember, they had kept some kind of fire going in that room all year round.

Of course, once Chester really got nasty about the divorce and Loetha's reluctance to agree to the settlement, he had succeeded in getting the power cut off more than once. Then, the fireplace had been the only source of warmth and hot water for Sylvia and her mother.

Coming around the last curve of the driveway, Sylvia slowed even more. If a person could ignore the washed out driveway and overlook the yard that hadn't been mowed at all since the last of August. And if a person could avoid worrying about the condition of the wood trim and the gutters, then Loetha's house still looked impressive. Yes, there was that one garage door on the three door garage that bowed sharply in the center, the oak panels splintered all the way across. But for as long as Loetha lived in the house, she'd probably never get that damage repaired.

Twenty feet from the back of the house, the housing development began. Before Chester had sold off that land, their backyard had opened out on a large field with a barn where Sylvia and her mother kept their horses. More than the infrequent rides that she and her mother took together, Sylvia remembered shoveling out the stalls. Loetha thought horseback riding would build Sylvia's poise and coordination. Cleaning out the stables was supposed to develop her character. They'd sold the horses soon after Chester had the power cut off the first time.

Making sure that Elaine's earflaps were tied under her chin, Sylvia took her hand and led her around the front of the house. They could have gotten inside quicker if they had gone through the garage, but the kitchen door inside the garage had warped or something. Loetha had called last night, trying to explain the problem to Brent. He'd told her he would send one of his mechanics over to see if he could fix it. But Sylvia knew that Loetha would have to call them three or four more times before Brent finally sent out one of his men. Her husband's generosity was always accompanied by a brooding regret.

Passing by the den's picture window, Sylvia saw her mother, gazing out, her arms crossed, one hand holding her afternoon mug of Russian tea and rum. By the time Sylvia had taken five more steps, Loetha had rushed out the front door of the house and scooped up Elaine.

"Mother, you're barefoot." Sylvia gave Loetha a gentle push back toward the front door.

Loetha slid her granddaughter onto her hip and glanced down. "Lord, I hope the neighbors don't find out."

Sylvia glanced around their front yard. It had returned to broom straw and white pine saplings. No wonder Brent thought he could get away with not mowing it but once every month or two in the summer. Grown up as it was, the yard still sloped down toward the barely visible highway with an elegance that Sylvia recognized as belonging to another time. Other people. She shook her head. In the backyard, or what was left of it, Loetha had a few hundred neighbors whose children and dogs were constantly bumping into her back windows and doors—at all hours. But the front yard still hung onto the estate that once graced the top of Coultrane Hill. Sylvia knew that one reason Brent came courting her was his dream of one day living in the house that Chester Coultrane built. Unfortunately, poor Brent didn't know and then later didn't want to believe that Chester Coultrane had already begun subdividing Coultrane Hill when he realized he could continue to assert his aristocracy, shack up with a younger woman, and still bank a respectable profit if he filled up the hill with prefabricated homes.

"How's my Lady Elaine?" Loetha glided an index finger along the fleecy edge of her granddaughter's earflap.

"I put on earmuffs and sat in a room all by myself so they could see if I could hear the birds." Elaine drooped over her grandmother's arm, an indication that she wanted to get down.

Knowing that her mother sometimes missed Elaine's signals, Sylvia took her daughter out of Loetha's arms and swung her to the floor, pointing her in the direction of the main hall. Elaine always wound up running down that long hall to Sylvia's old bedroom. She preferred sitting on Sylvia's canopy bed and playing with her mother's old dolls to being stroked by her grandmother. Sylvia kept waiting for her mother to say something about instilling in Elaine a stronger sense of family, but for the last four years, Loetha had been too preoccupied with her continuing battle with her ex-husband, his lawyers, and the death of Keith to start shaping Elaine into a Southern Belle.

"Elaine needs to get tubes put in her ears." As soon as her daughter had disappeared down the hall, Sylvia took the mug of Russian tea from her mother and sampled it. Loetha wasn't stirring in too much rum.

"Want me to fix you a cup?" Loetha took her mug from Sylvia and settled down on the couch that sat angled between the huge fireplace and the picture window.

The angle of the couch threw off the rest of the room's furnishings, but Loetha insisted on keeping it crooked because she spent most of her days watching for Chester or one of his thugs to sneak up and set the house on fire. Sylvia had tried to explain to her mother that Chester didn't need to stoop to felony to make her life miserable. It was much more satisfying for him to pry away his ex-wife's property and pride from her through legal channels.

Still, Sylvia could appreciate her mother's need for melodrama. She just had to keep her eye on Loetha's rum bottles. It was hard enough to convince Brent that his mother-in-law needed financial support until the divorce was finally settled. But if Brent suspected that Loetha was spending her allowance on alcohol, she could easily find herself back at the mercy of the plumbers and carpenters like she was back before Sylvia had married Brent.

"Mama, am I going to have to keep an eye on you like before?" Sylvia decided she could use a cup of tea–but without the rum. As she passed by her mother, Sylvia squeezed Loetha's knee. Its knobbiness made Sylvia think twice about leaving the rum out of her own drink. "I don't want to have to dry you out again."

For a moment, Loetha's eyes came into full focus on Sylvia's face. The way they once did when she was instructing her in the secrets of being a Southern Belle. "Lord, I never want to go through that again."

The kitchen was dark. It had triple windows over the sink, but Loetha kept the shutters locked on that side of the house. Twenty feet from the kitchen window, the housing development spread out in the distance, across what used to be their meadow, down into the small valley where Sylvia and Keith played in the creek when they were children, and up the hill on the other side. Cheap little houses as far as the eye could bear the ugliness. And Chester had sold all that land right out from under Loetha. There for three years, he had been raking in money while Sylvia and Loetha kept the windows covered, hiding from bill collectors. For days at a time, Loetha lay passed out in her bedroom.

From the den, Loetha called in her ragged voice, "When they going to put them tubes in Elaine's ears?"

Although the power had been turned back on after the first month that Sylvia had started dating Brent, neither she nor her mother had felt comfortable using the lights after all the unpleasantness the power company had caused them when they hadn't been able to pay the bill–all those years ago. At her own home, Sylvia felt only slightly uneasy using the electricity, but at her mother's house, she still worried that somebody in a yellow plastic hat would come knocking on the door if she flipped on a switch. Her mother was still using kerosene lamps. They'd gotten out of that financial trouble six years ago.

"Can't set a date for the surgery until I talk to Brent." Sylvia sat down on the couch beside her mother. "You know how cautious he can be."

"Oh, he just likes to hear people explain their needs." Loetha curved her shoulders inside the large flannel shirt that had belonged to Keith. "As much as he loves Elaine, he won't object to the tubes."

"Yes, he will." Sylvia lifted her cup to her lips and let the fragrance of the tea seep into her face. "He's got it in his head that the operation is more dangerous than ear infections two or three times a month."

"That sounds to me like he's considered the operation." Loetha rested her mug on her knee and gazed out the big window.

From the slack lines along her mother's mouth and the way Loetha's eyes seemed to flatten against the view of her tangled front yard, Sylvia knew her mother had closed the curtain around her brain. She sat rigidly on the couch, like a woman in a canoe too unstable to be on the water. Briefly, Sylvia wished her mother could be drunk and raging once again. If the scene would last for only two or three minutes, Sylvia wished she could see her mother and Keith, both drunk and shouting at the empty chair at the dining room table where Chester used to sit and talk about being wealthy and how lucky she and Keith were, being the children of a wealthy daddy. Keith was to take over the meat processing business and the rental property when he grew up. Sylvia was going to be the social leader of the whole town. Of course, as Chester saw it, she had to marry right.

Loetha's job had been to groom Sylvia. Teach her how to be a Southern Belle. Even if Sylvia had been better in school, her mother would still have made her take home economics, and then four times a week in the evenings, she had taken Sylvia to old Mrs. Harris's house to learn how to walk and sit and speak. She was supposed to be an ornament for the home of some doctor or lawyer. Or a businessman—if the business was respectable enough.

After she flunked out of modeling school, Sylvia had called home. Chester was supposedly gone on a business trip, so Keith had to come and pick her and her belongings up. Loetha had been too drunk to make the trip to Atlanta. Of course, Keith had been drunk too. Every trip he made from Sylvia's apartment out to the car was marked by a trail of dropped clothes or kitchen utensils. How he was able to drop spatulas and knives when Sylvia had taped them up in boxes simply confirmed for Sylvia how shattered her family life was about to become.

On the eight-hour drive back home from Atlanta, Keith had tried to make Sylvia forget that she had just dropped out of modeling school. "Okay, you won't be an ornament for some aristocrat's mansion." Keith paused long enough to light his cigarette, a chore that took several seconds because the cigarette lighter in the twelve-year-old Thunderbird got hot only in one small corner of the metal coil. So Keith had to rotate the lighter around the tip of his cigarette, as if he were chalking up a pool cue. When the cigarette finally smoked to life, Keith plugged the lighter back into the dashboard and tilted his head back against his seat. "With mine and mama's help, you can still develop the skills to at least be a major appliance in some lucky man's home."

Sylvia's mother inspected the button on the left sleeve of her shirt. She rocked the button in the light coming through her picture window. Then she rubbed her thumb across the button. Sylvia had grown up watching her mother check blouses and shirts button by button. On more than one occasion, she'd caught her mother double checking the teeth on zippers. In all of her life, Sylvia had never asked her mother why fasteners held such a fascination for her. But now, as the smoke of Loetha's acrimonious divorce seemed about to settle, Sylvia no longer felt irritated by her mother's scrutiny of where two pieces of cloth came together.

"You need to always consider your husband's point of view." Loetha rubbed her wrist where the cuff button touched it. "A Belle doesn't badger."

"That's where I always start, Mama." Sylvia stood up. She picked up her mother's empty mug. "But I was raised to move toward the sensible."

"You can move toward whatever you want." Loetha reached for the mug but then waved her daughter toward the kitchen. "Just don't try to drag your husband with you."

"Right now, I'll move toward the kitchen." Sylvia didn't ask her mother if she wanted another mug of tea. She wouldn't. Not until Sylvia left. And if it was a good day for Loetha, she might wait another two and a half hours and drink her tea with her supper. She'd be okay as long as some catastrophe didn't push her over the edge again.

Sylvia leaned around the corner to check on her mother. Did Loetha, she wondered, have any edges left? She dropped off the planet almost when Chester left her. Sylvia had wrestled her back to sobriety that time. In a way, Sylvia was grateful for the pure work required to dry her mother out. She hadn't been back from Atlanta too long. She'd sat right beside her mother twenty-four hours a day. On bad nights, she'd had to tumble dry her mother. Argue with her about all the people and creatures she thought were coming to get her.

When Chester started selling off the land behind the house when the divorce proceedings had just begun, when the first bulldozer clanked up through the meadow and knocked down the barn, Loetha had gone back to the rum. More than once, Sylvia had found her mother semi-conscious in a lawn chair in what was left of their backyard, watching the excavation for as long as her two children would let her. Keith had been some help. He was trying to start up a business with a friend of his, Jerry, selling rhododendron and laurel bushes in New Jersey. What few dollars Keith brought home from those trips helped keep them in peanut butter sandwiches, dill pickles, and coffee. To this day, Sylvia had never found out where her mother got the money for her rum.

Sylvia had wanted to believe that Jerry was growing all those bushes that they loaded on the back of a large flatbed truck and parked in some empty lot just outside of places like Patterson and Trenton where they'd sit and sell the shrubs to commuters driving Volvos and Hondas. But two or three nights before they'd leave for New Jersey, Keith always got restless and breathless, more excited than Sylvia could connect to simply loading a truck with a few hundred bushes.

That second time she tumble dried her mother out, she had already started getting visits from Brent Harper. She'd met him when, for a little relief from watching her mother, she'd ridden over to the truck dealership with Keith to get some work done on Jerry's flatbed truck. When Keith had asked her to come along for the ride, she'd wondered why he insisted that she fix herself up a little. At that time, only one of their eight toilets was working, and she'd been trying all that morning to unplug the one next to her mother's bedroom. At first, she refused to take Keith's request seriously, but finally, she realized that maybe she did need to shift to a lighter mood.

She and Keith pulled into the service department parking lot just as Brent Harper climbed out of his bronze Mercedes. Keith had yelled Brent's name then asked him how long he might have to wait before getting his truck worked on. Even though everybody in town knew about Chester and Loetha's divorce, nobody doubted that Keith Coultrane still stood closer than anybody to Chester's money. They were wrong. As Sylvia had known all along, Chester had given Keith a choice. When he chose to stay with his mother, Keith had as good as erased his attachment to his father all the way back to Chester's memory of his orgasm. Much of Chester's relentless dismantling of the family estate was aimed at punishing the son who had sided against him.

Between his mistaken belief that Keith might one day suddenly turn up rich and Sylvia's flirtatious attention, Brent Harper couldn't do enough for Keith's partner's flatbed truck. When one of the mechanics told Brent that he'd need the rest of the day to replace the transmission, Brent had offered to give Keith and Sylvia a ride home. Because of Sylvia's father's taste for large American cars, she had grown up familiar with Cadillacs and Lincolns, and she delighted Brent Harper when she told him he had been the first man to give her a ride in a Mercedes. That was all it took to get him coming by three and four times a week, just to give her the thrill of riding in his Mercedes.

"What's a man good for if not to show a good-looking woman a good time?" Brent had once asked Sylvia after that first month of driving her all over the state.

Not too long after Sylvia let Brent marry her, he told her that he had to buy her a car to drive herself around in. She had accepted that gift about two weeks before he discovered how much it was going to cost him to buy his mother-in-law out of debt. But what were daughters for, Sylvia asked herself as she stood up from the couch to go check on Elaine, if not to help their mothers any way they could?

And what were sons for? Sylvia wondered as she made her way down the long hall to her room at the other end of the house. It was dark because her mother kept the bedroom doors closed. Her father had never been clear about why he wanted a house with eight bedrooms when only four people lived there. Sylvia knew better than to ask her mother if earlier on in her married life she was expecting to have more than two children. Back in Sylvia's earliest memory of her mother discussing the facts of life, Loetha had equated love with submitting to the husband.

On their honeymoon, Brent had admitted to Sylvia that he had a dream of making love to her in all eight bedrooms of her mother's house. That ambition had sounded a muffled alarm in Sylvia's brain. Even her mother had stopped sleeping in her and Chester's bedroom. Except for her own room, all the other bedrooms crowded against visitors like trophy rooms too full of stuffed animal heads. Not one room actually contained a stuffed animal, but somehow, Chester Coultrane had put the stamp of his ego on every piece of furniture and that mark made every chair, every couch, every nightstand cower like creatures who have had their spirits yanked out and replaced with foam rubber or wads of cotton.

The hall was also dark because all five of the hall lights were burned out. For a second, Sylvia had to lean against the wall when she remembered that the last person who replaced those light bulbs was Keith. The night before he had gone out to pick up a load of bushes to take up to New Jersey. About three hours after Keith had left, Sylvia thought he and his partner were long gone. Keith told Sylvia while he was replacing the light bulbs that this trip would be the first to show enough profit to put him in a position to pay some of the bigger bills weighing down his mother's house. Some landscaper they'd talked to on their last trip to New Jersey wanted to buy three times their usual load.

Having to hide from bill collectors during the day, Sylvia had become a creature of the night. At least when the sun went down, men were less likely to be dropping by to deliver ugly messages from everybody they owed money to. In a way, Sylvia was relieved that their phone had been cut off. At least that line of communication had been denied the collection agencies. Keith told Sylvia that they didn't have to tolerate those visits, but he was away so much that his indignation felt hollow to Sylvia. Her mother had the right idea: just keep the shutters closed, the curtains drawn, and not answer the door.

That particular night, as Sylvia was beginning her sixteenth or seventeenth game of solitaire, she'd heard a car bumping up their driveway. After a couple of seconds, Sylvia realized it certainly wasn't Brent Harper coming to keep her company. This vehicle moved along with an unmuffled growl. As it roared up the driveway, Sylvia could hear chunks of asphalt being thrown up, clattering in two and three wheel wells at a time. Whoever approached her mother's house was moving fast. Much sooner than she thought possible, the sound of the engine echoed against the garage side of the house and then Sylvia heard the sound of a garage door being smashed. The whole den vibrated and three spiky chunks of plaster fell from the ceiling.

From where she'd been sleeping on the couch, Loetha raised her head. "What the Lord was that?" Although this was Loetha's second period of being dried out, her sleep-soaked reflexes tended more to muffle her from stimulation than to make her more attuned.

Before Loetha had finished asking her question, Sylvia had opened the kitchen door and peeked out into the garage. The flatbed truck's headlights were angled enough toward the wall opposite the kitchen door that Sylvia wasn't blinded by their glare. Enough light bounced back into the windshield of the truck that she recognized Keith slumped over the steering wheel.

Not wanting to alarm her mother and definitely not wanting any groggy help, Sylvia waved her hand in her mother's direction. "It's just Keith. He's bumped the garage door with his truck."

Loetha rolled over and burrowed her forehead into the couch. "Why can't he do that in New Jersey where it won't disturb people?"

Pausing at the door just long enough to make sure Loetha was asleep, Sylvia stepped out into the garage. She had to stoop slightly to affirm her suspicion that Keith hadn't moved in the two or three minutes he'd been sitting there at the wheel. Even during his heaviest drinking, Keith never kept himself draped over a steering wheel this long. He didn't like being in cars when he was drinking. He once told Sylvia that the world had a tendency to spin unexpectedly when he was drinking, and he couldn't drive or even sit in a car during those times of geographical uncertainty.

When she got to the driver's door, she heard Keith groan. What Sylvia saw in the dim light of the truck's overhead bulb after she opened the door made her groan. Keith was covered with blood. His hair was sticky with it. His shirt clung to his skin. She noticed that part of his back looked as if something had been chewing on it.

Cupping her hand under Keith's jaw, she gently raised his head. "What happened?"

Keith opened his eyes and tried to turn his head toward Sylvia. But he could move only far enough to stare at the headlights shining against the garage wall. "Some old man shot me."

"Lord, God, Keith." Sylvia glanced at the kitchen door. There was a disconnected phone right inside the door. "Was he trying to steal your bushes?" She saw that the back of the truck was carrying barely a quarter load of azaleas.

Keith took a careful, shallow breath, drooping his head heavily against Sylvia's palm. "We was stealing *his* bushes."

Keeping her palm steady under her brother's jaw, Sylvia slid onto the seat beside him. "I got to get you some help."

"Do it easy, Sis." Keith shuddered as Sylvia pushed him from under the steering wheel.

With her free hand, Sylvia started the truck. "You want to lean against me or against the door?"

"Stay where I am." Keith managed to pull his jaw off of Sylvia's hand and let his head loll against her shoulder. He flopped his right hand toward the passenger door. "Don't want to get that far from family."

Easing over the potholes in the driveway, Sylvia could feel her brother's body tighten with each bump. She wanted the noise coming from his throat to be "bump, bump, bump," but she knew he wasn't saying that. She could feel her shoulder warming with Keith's blood.

"Did Jerry get shot too?" She pulled out onto the smooth pavement of the highway. She wasn't really interested in what Keith might say just so long as he would stop making that noise in his throat.

"He took off into the woods when the first barrel knocked me on my face." Unexpectedly, Keith raised his head from Sylvia's shoulder like he might ask her to pull over and let him drive the rest of the way to the hospital.

Sylvia wiped her eyes and felt her cheeks get sticky from her hand. "All for a load of bushes that don't bloom more than two weeks a year."

Keith tilted his head back and took another shallow breath. "But we could get at least thirty dollars a bush in New Jersey."

"You shouldn't get shot like this, just for stealing a few squatty little bushes."

"Sylvia, you ought to know that we must have stole bushes about six different times from this old man's property." Keith let his head ease back onto his sister's shoulder.

"Well, I'm going to let you explain all of it to Mother." Sylvia reached up and steadied his head.

In the emergency room, Sylvia thought she would have to settle down for a long wait, but before she had time to notice that other people in the waiting room were staring at her bloody clothes, one of the doctors who had wheeled Keith off down a tile hallway had run back to Sylvia and told her to come with him. Keith had told them he was dying, and the three doctors agreed. So for fifteen minutes, Sylvia sat on a metal stool, holding her brother's hand, listening to his punctured lungs. When his breathing stopped sounding so painful and full of struggle, Sylvia stood up and hugged him.

His hand brushed her elbow. "That's what I needed."

"Don't be afraid." Sylvia pulled away enough to look at his face.

"I'm not." Keith looked around the room then back at Sylvia. "You're the one who's got to deal with Mother."

"I don't know what I'll say."

"Tell her it was a gardening accident." Keith looked out over Sylvia's head and kept on looking.

In the bedroom, Sylvia saw that Elaine had fallen asleep. The medicine she took for her congestion made her sleepy, prone to drop off at the dinner table, in front of the television, and sometimes even in bed. Lying there, surrounded by her mother's old dolls and stuffed animals, Elaine looked slightly smaller than life-size herself, more vulnerable than ever to germs, to housing developments, and to fathers' misdirected frustration or crooked protectiveness. For a few moments, Sylvia felt afraid for her daughter. Cold with the knowledge of what a woman had to do if she wanted to keep the plumbers and the electricians and the doctors and the truck dealership owners happy. She spread a blanket over Elaine and thought about going back to the den to stand beside the fireplace.

As she backed from the bed, though, she noticed that Elaine had opened the curtains and the afternoon sun slanted through the windows, the dust motes floating around in the beam like carbonation in a bottle of ginger ale. The light claimed a wavy square of the carpet about two feet from the bed. In the center of the square of light, Sylvia noticed four evenly spaced indentations in the pile of the carpet. Not having to make any mental connections, she pulled her white wicker chair from her desk at the foot of her bed and slid it over to the four dimples in the light. The four legs of the chair fit perfectly into the indentations.

Sylvia sat down in the chair, feeling the sunlight touch her skin, warm as the blood of her brother. Warm as her own blood. Warming it up more than a woman's blood should be. Years before, she had sat in this exact place, mostly on those days when she had missed school. And because she had to be the Southern Belle for her mother and father, she sat in her room before all of them came home, collecting in the den or the kitchen, expecting her to assure them, warm away their fear. Like she was an iron, and only she could smooth away the wrinkles in their lives.

That was all anybody wanted from her, Sylvia realized. She soaked up more of the sunlight. How long had she gone without feeling this warm? This capable of comfort? Along the full length of her neck, she felt her pulse turning to radiance, her blood lighting up all the chilly caverns and dark tubes inside her. What became perfectly clear to her was that a man who had been brave enough to marry into her life could be shown he had nothing to fear from minor surgery. She had plenty enough heat to make that crease disappear.

Women Like Islands

In the summer of 1980, Nelly Shoun found herself in Honolulu, waiting for her fiancé to finish his book on sumo wrestling so he could move on to marrying her. They had met a
year and a half ago when Porter was finishing his book about
professional women wrestlers: *Maids of the Mat.*

At that time, Nelly had just about worked her way to the
top ranks of women wrestlers in the Appalachian Wrestling
Alliance, a small franchise that included the mountainous parts
of Kentucky, Tennessee, North Carolina, Virginia, Georgia,
and Pennsylvania. Had Nelly not already suspected that being
a wrestler was turning her into a woman she couldn't live with,
she might not have let herself fall in love with Porter Lambert.
Had Nelly not fallen in love with Porter Lambert, she would
have migrated, in a couple of years, to Charlotte and the big
league: the NWA. The National Wrestling Alliance.

Not five months after she had crossed the line from being
a baby face–a good wrestler–to being a heel–a bad wrestler–as
Nasty Nelly, the Cherokee Banshee, she'd been visited by promoters from the NWA and the WWF. But as soon as Nelly
found out that she'd have to move to New York City to join
the WWF, she had stopped listening to their representative.
She actually dreaded when the time came for her to make the

move up in her profession. She was perfectly happy, living in Asheville. Well, as happy as anyone could be who was having to fight on average three times a week to make a living.

As Nelly pedaled from the pedicab garage, she already had a clear idea which hotel she would park in front of while she waited for customers. The day before, she had overheard two of her customers talking about a hula demonstration taking place in the lobby of the Royal Hawaiian. Although Nelly had now been on Oahu for a month and five days, she still wasn't used to the heat. Certainly, she was more tanned than she'd ever been in her life, but her metabolism refused to settle down into what she hoped would be a calmer island rhythm. As far as Nelly was concerned, those people who kept reassuring her that the Oahu breezes would keep her comfortable were the same kind of people who reasssured her that she didn't need to worry about sharks when she was in the ocean. All the breezes that Nelly had come in contact with probed instead of refreshed, poking at Nelly as if not quite certain what she was made of.

In the ten minutes she had taken to pedal her rickshaw bicycle to the Royal Hawaiian from the pedicab garage, where she paid her ten dollar a day rental fee, Nelly's green and blue aloha shirt was already damp under her arms and down the full length of her spine. She knew she'd probably be cooler if she dressed like the other pedicab drivers: net tank tops, flimsy nylon running shorts . . . . Some of the more enterprising female pedicab drivers even wore French cut bikinis. But Nelly suspected they were in the business for love as much as for money. The single men who hired the bikini drivers gave huge tips, but Nelly had no intention of letting her butt become part of the Waikiki scenery.

Besides, Nelly knew she was too big to make big tips—either from the single men on vacation or from the elderly couples who were too afraid of the surfer boys who generally drove the pedicabs around Honolulu. Old people liked her as their driver because at 6' 1" and 230 pounds, she looked strong enough to pedal them around town without hurting herself. In her oversized Hawaiian shirts, her pleated fatigue shorts, and her crisp white running shoes, she struck most tourists as exotic, strong, and dependable. More like some Polynesian yak than a Pacific flower. Unfortunately, most elderly tourists weren't generous tippers.

If these people had only seen a few of Nelly's later wrestling matches, shortly before she retired, they wouldn't have so happily climbed into the springy little passenger seat of her pedicab. She had been merciless in the ring once she became Nasty Nelly the Cherokee Banshee. When one of the promoters of the Appalachian Wrestling Alliance had offered to pay her an extra three hundred dollars a match if she would perform some maneuver off the top rope, she had become the first woman in the AWA to do a half-flip from the top ring post, splashing with her back onto the abdomen of her prostrate opponent. Although she had taken the move from the Mexican cruiser weight wrestlers, the Luche Libres, who had probably stolen it from the Japanese wrestlers, Nelly had added a tomahawk chop to her victim's sternum as she landed. She had named her move the Cherokee Sunset.

Not long after she'd introduced the Cherokee Sunset, Nelly had found herself in a bout that got uglier than she or the promoters had planned. Her opponent was a veteran who went by the name of Irish Rose. She was a stocky woman, maybe ten inches shorter than Nelly. But she dyed her hair red then teased it up about a foot high. She also had two large shamrocks, nearly five inches across, tattooed between her collarbones and her breasts. She'd been drinking before the match–later, Nelly found out she'd been left by her husband–and had no intention of following the loose choreography that she and Nelly had worked up a few days earlier.

At one point in the match, Irish Rose was supposed to throw Nelly over the top rope while the referee wasn't looking. But instead of falling down to the gymnasium floor, Nelly was going to catch the back of Irish Rose's head and run her nose along the rope. Not in the mood to have her nose run along the rope, Irish Rose punched Nelly in the ear as she reached for the back of her head. Furious from the unexpected pain and losing her balance on the narrow apron of the ring, Nelly gabbed two handsful of Irish Rose's red hair as she half fell and half jumped down to the floor. Of course, Nelly expected Irish Rose's head to bounce back after it hit the springy top rope, but she forgot to let go of Irish Rose's hair.

When she landed on the floor, standing, with her arms stretched toward the rafters of the building, Nelly saw that she was holding two large hanks of red hair. Immediately, the announcers at ringside started referring to the move as the Banshee Scalp. In later matches, when Nelly was supposed to use the Banshee Scalp, her opponents came to the ring wearing falls. Her more professional opponents, when they knew they were scheduled to be scalped during the match would even go so far as to have two spots on their heads shaved so Nelly's scalping would appear even more dramatic.

Seven other pedicabs were parked in the unloading zone in front of the hotel, so Nelly rode on by the entrance about a third of a block then casually backed toward the front doors, keeping an eye on the pedicab driver behind her, watching for signs of hostility. For the most part, pedicab drivers weren't territorial, but Nelly wanted to avoid any risk of provoking one of the other drivers who might be having a bad day or who was coming off a bad night.

Actually, Nelly worried more about being provoked than being provoking. Given enough hostile stimulation, Nelly could cross into a temper that took over her mind and body like a hurricane taking over a circus tent. Early on in her wrestling career, the promoters had seen how she could lose control. More than most wrestler's ring names, Nasty Nelly did announce a deep truth about Nelly Shoun's identity.

The small time promoters who guided the wrestlers in the Appalachian Wrestling Alliance encouraged Nelly to develop and display what made her Nasty Nelly. As a *heel*, they told her, a big part of the job was to make sure the fans hated her. In fact, her opponents in the ring were only a third of her job. When she was wrestling, she was expected to abuse her opponent *and* insult the audience. When she wasn't wrestling, she was still expected to insult the fans. As a person who had never distinguished herself in any social or academic activity, Nelly had been astounded to discover just how good she was at provoking wrestling fans.

If she hadn't met Porter, she might have forgotten that she was Nelly Shoun long before she had started becoming Nasty Nelly. When he first interviewed her, she gave all her answers as Nasty Nelly. To all reporters, Nelly recited the same story of her life–as imagined by the publicists who worked for the AWA. She had grown up on the Cherokee Reservation in western North Carolina. Her family was poor and had to sell souvenirs to the tourists. The poverty and the shame had driven her father to alcoholism and her mother to despair. She had escaped from the reservation to make the world pay for what it had done to her family.

Dutifully, Porter had written down everything that Nelly said. At the end of the interview, he had asked her to have lunch with him. Because Nelly had received very clear instructions from the management to cooperate with this reporter, she accepted his offer. Though used to giving interviews to individual reporters and comfortable with infuriating a few hundred fans at a time, Nelly felt uncomfortable sitting across the table from Porter. He wasn't an imposing person. He was about thirty. Five years older than Nelly. His hair was thinning in the front. While his shoulders weren't exactly narrow, they definitely weren't broad. Any one of the women in the gym could probably pin Porter inside of three minutes.

But when he started talking to her over lunch, Nelly couldn't keep herself from liking him. He talked about *Maids of the Mat*. Very soon, Nelly realized that Porter could see around the lives the managers and promoters had concocted for their clients, but he didn't accuse anyone of lying to him.

"I'm writing the book for the fans. And your bosses know what the fans want to hear." Porter tore off a piece of the aluminum foil which had been partially wrapped around the sea bass he'd ordered. "The publisher wants to please the readers—not challenge them." He folded the piece of aluminum into a pair of tiny sunglasses and put them on the fish's head. When he saw that Nelly was staring at how he'd decorated his fish, he adjusted the small glasses to cover the fish's accusing eye. "I love sea bass, but I can't stand to have them watch me eat."

More than handsome, more than macho, Porter was calm. Which wasn't to say he was dull. He wasn't calm like a nap. He was calm like a massage after a day-long workout, after a ten-hour road trip. He was a calm that reminded Nelly of who she had once been. Back before she was Nasty, back before she was even Cherokee.

The familiar din of an audience dissolving into an exiting crowd pulled Nelly's attention back to the front doors of the Royal Hawaiian. The hula demonstration was letting out.

Nelly climbed off her bicycle and stood beside it, her hand gripping the seat. Most of the other pedicab drivers didn't bother to dismount when customers approached. With two weeks of experience, Nelly understood why some drivers didn't dismount. As soon as customers began climbing into the back seat of the pedicab, the driver had to keep both front and back brakes locked to prevent the pedicab from swishing around. But Nelly felt more comfortable greeting strangers when she didn't have to straddle a metal frame.

If Porter's advance for the sumo book hadn't started evaporating so quickly under the weight of Hawaiian rent and food prices, Nelly would have preferred not to work with the public. Her life as Nasty Nelly had begun to make her distrustful of strangers, especially if those strangers were part of an audience she was being paid to antagonize. However, all the jobs that Nelly had considered, inside jobs, served only to emphasize her size. On her way to see about construction jobs, Nelly had paused to let a pedicab cross in front of her. The driver was saying something to his two passengers about Waikiki, and they were nodding, in rhythm to the sway of the pedicab, as if they might fall asleep.

After five years of being interviewed and after a year and a half of living with a man who made his living conducting interviews, Nelly had no trouble striking up a conversation with the next pedicab driver she met. He pointed out the hotel garage where any strong-legged person could walk up and rent a pedicab for ten dollars a day up front. Despite not being the type who got the big tips, Nelly had been able to make almost six hundred dollars since she'd started.

Many of the people walking by Nelly's pedicab were laughing or trying to do hula movements as they walked. Nelly could tell that they were too preoccupied with what they had just seen to notice her and her pedicab. Several people who did catch sight of Nelly cut off their laughter and inspected her as if they thought she might try to sell them an old fish. That kind of inspection didn't bother Nelly. She kept her back straight and tried to slap the people with her own sidelong inspection—always much briefer and more disapproving than those frisking her dimensions.

Then, out of the hotel came the largest woman that Nelly had ever seen. She was probably four or five inches taller than Nelly and at least thirty pounds heavier. She was dressed in a muumuu so red that her shadow was purple on the sidewalk. On her head, she wore a wreath of ferns. Her wrists and ankles were also wrapped in ferns. In her right hand, she carried a large gourd. In her left hand, she carried a larger, double gourd that resembled a tremendous hourglass. These two gourds amplified the woman's size.

For the few moments that Nelly studied her, the Hawaiian woman stood in the center of a crowd of people. Behind the woman—on the outer edge of the crowd—stood two Hawaiian men and three other women, all of them only slightly smaller than the woman in red. Twice as she was signing autographs, the large woman scowled toward Nelly. Each time, Nelly checked her shirt and shorts to see what the woman could be finding so offensive about her. After ten minutes of watching the woman sign autographs, her five companions moved closer to the crowd, squeezing people out of their way. It wasn't the most discreet crowd control that Nelly had seen, but it was effective. Further hinting that the Hawaiian woman was finished satisfying her fans, a dark limousine pulled up in front of the hotel.

By now, Nelly was the last pedicab driver parked in front of the crowd. When the limousine nosed its way next to the curb, she had to push her pedicab out of the way. In the few seconds she had to concentrate on getting her bike moved and lined up with the sidewalk, the Hawaiian woman had said something to disperse the remaining fans who tried to ignore her large companions. Then, after a brief conversation with those companions, the woman had gestured them into the wide doors of the limousine and waved with her double gourd as the car drifted into the traffic.

As soon as the limousine disappeared, the Hawaiian woman fastened her eyes on Nelly and walked straight toward her. Although the street was crowded, the woman choreographed her progress so that neither she nor the people she crossed in front of had to change the speed of their walking. Returning the woman's stare, Nelly felt her shoulders and thighs tensing the way they did just before her first lock up when a wrestling match had begun. She kept one hand on her bicycle seat but tugged her shirt free from her sticky back.

"So, you're driving a cab." The woman stopped a few feet in front of Nelly. Her voice was soft, still carrying over the noise of the street, deep and accusing.

Now that the woman was standing closer, Nelly noticed that the woman's hair was so black that it reflected blue light. Her hands dwarfed the large gourds she still carried. Realizing the size of the woman's hands, Nelly glanced down at her feet and saw that they were bare and gigantic. Again, Nelly gazed back at the woman's face. It was broad with wide-set, dark eyes. This was the closest Nelly had ever stood to an authentic Hawaiian, probably island aristocracy.

The woman allowed Nelly to appraise her as if she expected it, but the appraisal apparently took longer than it should have because she moved just a couple of feet from Nelly. "Instead of a tour, why don't you give me a ride home?"

No longer adjusting her shirt, Nelly kept her hand behind her back because she didn't want the woman to know she had a fist bouquet to present to her if she moved one foot closer. This woman wasn't asking for a ride home–she was *demanding* one. Nelly was amused and breathless. The woman was big, probably strong, and royal. Used to getting her way. For a moment, the woman's presence appeared to Nelly as a challenge. Deep in her own core, Nelly felt the grapple lust flicker. After all, wrestling had never been about competition for Nelly. It had been about curiosity: not about who would win but about what the opponents would do to each other before the match ended.

Almost as soon as Nelly detected that dark anticipation, she tried to slump away from it, arching her back and taking a step away from the large woman. She had run away from wrestling to escape the perverse joy that came with riding her anger into and over another human being. Nasty Nelly the Cherokee Banshee scared her. She had run away with Porter because he knew Nasty Nelly but didn't encourage her to make public appearances–or even private ones for that matter. Nelly had run away to Hawaii because it sounded like a peaceful place to be. Didn't Pacific mean peaceful, after all? What did Hawaii mean? Nelly wondered. It had to be something soothing as well.

"I'll need directions." Nelly stepped to the side and nodded toward the passenger seat. She thought about giving the woman help getting in. Then she realized the best help she could provide was to keep the brakes on so the bike wouldn't roll as the woman climbed into the seat.

Barely giving Nelly time to mount the bike and squeeze the brakes, the large woman stepped upon the small running board, spun herself around, and slid into the seat. She didn't groan or giggle like most of Nelly's passengers. But even more surprising to Nelly, the large woman didn't shoot the usual tremors through the frame of the pedicab the way some people half her size usually did.

"I live at Hibiscus Plaza, just below Na Laau Arboretum. All you do is follow Kalakaua Avenue until it turns into Diamond Head Road. Think you can do that, Miss Pedicab?"

Getting started was so difficult that Nelly couldn't reply. She had to clench her teeth, strain up against the handlebars, and shift all of her weight onto one pedal, then the other pedal. It was the kind of effort that must have cranked the earth toward its first rotation. Laboriously, Nelly wobbled away from the curb. She hoped she wouldn't have to climb any of the hilly streets that surrounded Diamond Head. Kalakaua Avenue was level enough, running the entire length of Waikiki.

Except for late evening, traffic was heaviest around lunch time. Usually, passengers would fret about how close the cars were coming to their pedicab. Today's passenger, however, said nothing. Silence was fine with Nelly. Even on level ground, she could feel an oxygen deficiency blooming. It was a tiny flame behind her solar plexus. With very slight coaxing, this tiny flame could migrate, transform to that grapple lust she'd felt earlier. To halt her slide toward anger, Nelly glanced over her shoulder, hoping that some human physical frailty in the woman might help cool her temper. Each time Nelly looked back at her passenger, she was staring directly into her eyes. The woman was angry, but it was an anger that didn't seem to quite fit the woman's large proportions.

Once they crossed Kapahulu Avenue, a little over three miles from downtown Honolulu, they were officially out of Waikiki and entering Kapiolani Park. Nelly had come this way several times before, bringing people to the Honolulu Zoo, but she couldn't remember ever feeling as tired as she did now. The woman must have been heavier than she first calculated. Trying to distract herself from a cramp haunting her right calf and the dampness spreading down the waistband of her shorts, Nelly tried to recall if any other passengers who rode as couples had gotten her this tired after only three miles. As she struggled past Prince Kuhio Beach, she tried to remember ever having seen *any* heavy person riding one of the pedicabs. Maybe they were too self-conscious. The passenger seats couldn't be comfortable—certainly not as comfortable as the seats in a limousine.

Amplifying the woman's physical weight was the distinct disapproval Nelly felt rising from the woman like a vapor. All of it drifting across Nelly's shoulders, condensing around her lower back. This wasn't the gauzy tingle she used to feel when she'd managed to outrage an audience by some dirty wrestling maneuver or an especially low comment about the city where she was wrestling. This woman's disapproval was heavy on Nelly because it was personal. Like a mother's disapproval.

But Nelly had no mother. In her whole life, she'd had three families: she and Porter for a year and a half, the Appalachian Wrestling Alliance for five years, and the Mountain Meadow Home for Children for eighteen years. She'd been brought to the home as an infant. Had learned to walk on the polished wood floors in the dorm. Not too long after she'd taken her first step, she had twenty-two brothers and eighteen sisters who started teaching her how to wrestle. Every game they played at Mountain Meadow involved some element of physical force. One group of kids dominating all the other groups.

As far as Nelly could remember, the fights at Mountain Meadow were never frightening to her. In fact, they had always struck her as very intense, complex rituals of affection. No *individual* child was allowed to intimidate the weaker children. At the moment someone started acting like a genuine bully, all the other children combined against him or her. Though it was never discussed, the possibility of someone deliberately turning the daily tussles into occasions for serious injury or coercive assaults disturbed most of the children more deeply than the fact that they were orphans. As long as an assault was launched out of pure joy, it would be tolerated, encouraged, even organized so that as many people as possible could participate. Never tolerated was the solitary and arbitrary authority represented by a bully. It had been an ideal childhood as far as Nelly could tell.

Although Nelly had become one of the unchallenged leaders of the shifting confederations the children formed from day to day, she had never been tempted to be a leader. She liked people too much. Her natural inclination was to give people what they wanted. Then three years as a professional villain wrestler had twisted her way of thinking around to believe that most people wanted to be enraged and insulted. To have believed that perversion enough to make it her daily work, Nelly feared that she might have become just as twisted as her audience.

"We're about halfway there, Miss Pedicab." The woman's voice mixed with Nelly's sweat. Made it feel more salty, the kind of nauseating sweat that popped out on her forehead when she'd been punched too hard in the stomach.

A breeze chased after her, like a small dog hungry for her ankles. This wind seemed to be siding with the large Hawaiian woman as if it were part of her baffling scorn. Like her weight, the breeze dragged against Nelly's skin like an interrogation.

Nelly didn't speak because she didn't want to reveal how out of breath she was. Off to her left, she could see men playing cricket. Regular matches were held in the park. She liked their white uniforms. They were almost like suits. Always looked so cool. Her shirt now plastered itself to her ribs and waist.

Once again, she glanced over her shoulder at her passenger. She still wore a scowl which made the woman's broad face seem even broader. Brooding enough to sour a hog's stomach. Nelly thought about how satisfying it would be to stop the pedicab, grab the woman in a headlock, and squeeze that face back to a more pleasant width. With the thought came a spurt of adrenalin that made Nelly even more light-headed. She really wouldn't be happy if she remolded the woman's expression. Might even wind up getting herself and Porter exiled from Oahu. Maybe from all the islands.

"Here, take the left on Poni Moi Road." Now the woman's voice had become casual, but it still continued to sting Nelly. It was the sand at the beach during the day, bland to the point of being too hot to tolerate.

Important to remember why she had come to these islands. Certainly not to fight with the remains of the original people. Not one of the royal women who was so important that she could ride in a limousine. The woman had a power, Nelly admitted, which should have made her calm. But here she was pouting like a Polynesian prima donna. No. Nelly didn't want to work herself up. Up until she'd left Mountain Meadow Home for Children, she thought she had been calm. Oh, she had lost her temper on occasion when she was growing up, but what orphan at the home didn't?

Maybe it was the place itself that had helped Nelly grow up calm. She liked the food at the orphanage. She liked the house parents. Even the chores. Most of all, she had liked the grounds of the orphanage. It had been built on a meadow from the gray stones that had tumbled down from the higher slopes of the mountains. Later, when Nelly was eleven or twelve, the orphanage had sold tons of the gray rocks to a developer who used them to build, twenty miles up the road, modest castles in Scottish Hills–the most exclusive housing development in the whole county.

In one corner of the orphanage's meadow, a small lake had formed at the base of one of the area's matronly slopes. Nelly still thought of it as her lake even though she hadn't floated in it for almost seven years. Though not much of a swimmer, Nelly had always been a natural floater. What she counted as her calmest moments she now realized had occurred when she lay floating in that tingling cool water, watching clouds float above her. At those moments, she had no more substance, no more weight, no more anger than a puff of summer cloud.

As Nelly feared, this street was steep. She pulled herself out of the seat and stiffened her legs against the pedals to begin the climb. She tried not to think about the back of her pedicab with its heavy passenger and her disapproval. Each time she heaved her weight down onto the pedals, she could feel her calves turning incandescent, a groan trying to climb up out of her throat.

"Turn right." The woman's tone was cooler now. Almost purely informational as if she had detected Nelly's growing anger. "This is Hibiscus Drive."

With relief, Nelly saw that she would be able to get some rest. Hibiscus Drive sloped into a small valley at the roots of Diamond Head. She sat down on her seat and tried silently to catch her breath.

At the bottom of the street, the woman said, "Turn left."

This street climbed another hill, but it wasn't as steep as the one that Nelly had climbed earlier. As she prepared herself for the exertion, she let her eyes follow the dry gray sides of the crater looming over her. Although Diamond Head wasn't nearly as high as the mountains to the north, it seemed more isolated. In contrast to the Koolau Mountains, which reminded Nelly of the Appalachians with their fog and almost daily rainfall, Diamond Head rose starkly from the blue ocean to endure the uninterrupted glare of the sky.

That was how this passenger made Nelly feel. Her sympathy was definitely with the crater today even though it was partially responsible for the hill she was now trying to ascend. Nelly thought she knew how exposed the crater must feel under the disapproving scrutiny of the sun. She had to stop looking at Diamond Head in order to crouch more tightly over the handlebars of her bicycle. She squinted through the burn of her sweat. Her hands and heart felt welded to the metal of the pedicab. If she could have freed one hand to wipe the sweat out of her eyes, she wouldn't have.

Just as the flame in her calves and thighs was about to transform her bones to avocado pulp, Nelly heard the woman say, "The house at the end of the street, Miss Pedicab."

Through the palms in the yard, whose swaying strongly echoed the motion passing over Nelly's internal organs, she saw a sprawling stucco house with a roof the color of jade. Uncertain of her own contact with the physical world at the moment, Nelly couldn't determine just how many acres the house and its manicured lawn occupied. Sitting at the base of Diamond Head, the house shimmered like the mirage of some oasis, its greens flinging themselves against the gray crater with the brownish bushes clinging to its sides.

Not caring if she was pulling into the driveway of a mirage or a real house, Nelly was simply grateful that the pavement stayed level. To keep her legs from cramping, Nelly pulled herself off the seat and steadied her bicycle as best she could by holding onto the frame. The less she said to this woman, the better. Forget about discussing the fare. At this point, the kindest thing Nelly might say to her would be a warning. She knew this woman wouldn't take any word of caution for what it was meant to be. Soon as the woman climbed out, Nelly planned to remount and pedal off. She could get the rest she needed when she got to the bottom of Hibiscus Plaza.

"Well, you may not have any pride," the woman said as she climbed out of the cab. "But you've got strength."

"And it took every bit of what strength I had to pedal your heavy butt home." Speaking was difficult because Nelly's mouth was so dry. Fighting the pain snapping along the back of her legs, Nelly hopped stiffly back onto the bicycle seat and pushed off, thinking she would just leave the woman standing with her gourds in the driveway. But before she had moved two feet, she heard the hollow thump and rattle of the gourds being dropped on the ground. Then the bicycle stopped with such a jerk that Nelly almost went over the handlebars. The large woman had grabbed hold of the back of the passenger seat and stared over it. The rest of her face contorted with fury, the woman's eyes wavered with disbelief.

"It's bad enough that you degrade us in the streets of Waikiki, but how can you call yourself a Hawaiian and be so disrespectful of me, Kaahumanu. Or have you forgotten how important the hula is to us. Without me, our children would be learning the hula at the Holiday Inn and performing it in the bars."

Nelly had heard of the woman. For a moment, her temper cooled down. To be mistaken for a Hawaiian by Hawaiian royalty had to be some kind of honor. Sliding off her seat, Nelly twisted around to get a better view of the woman. "I'm not Hawaiian . . . ."

Before Nelly could tell the woman where she came from, the woman had ducked out of sight behind the passenger seat. When she raised back up, she had retrieved the two gourds she had dropped a few seconds earlier.

"*Don't* deny your home!" The woman threw the smaller of the two gourds at Nelly.

Amazed by the woman's insistence that she was Hawaiian, Nelly didn't get her hand up in time to block the gourd. It bounced off her forehead and transferred a large portion of its rattle to Nelly's brain. From the lowest parts of her anatomy, Nelly felt the grapple lust flare, anger caressing her jaw like scalding ruffles.

"You touch me or this bicycle one more time, and I'll push your face two feet deep into the front yard of your *home*." Nelly dragged her leg across the bar of the bicycle and whirled around to confront the Hawaiian woman.

She'd barely regained her balance when the woman threw the larger, double gourd at her. Riding her full temper now, Nelly's reflexes crested. She caught the gourd, hooking its narrow middle between her thumb and index finger. For the first time since she'd seen the large woman, Nelly detected a weakness. The double gourd meant something to her. That was all that Nasty Nelly needed to know. Keeping her gaze on the woman's eyes, Nelly grasped the rounded ends of the gourd in the palms of each hand and snapped it in half. She heard seeds pinging on the pavement.

When the Hawaiian woman saw Nelly emptying the seeds from the broken gourd, she let out a yell, deep and gutteral, then charged toward Nelly. At the time Nelly had dismounted from the bicycle, she had deliberately gotten off so she was standing next to the lawn in front of the woman's house. In the unlikely event that the woman would take her down, Nelly didn't want to be skidding around on the pavement. During the brief seconds the woman took to reach her, Nelly moved onto the soft grass of the woman's yard.

Had the woman come at Nelly intending to grab her, Nelly planned to hip toss her. It was a smooth move that wouldn't take much energy, just grab the woman's dress with both hands, step a little to the inside of the woman's direction, throw her own butt into the woman's lower abdomen, and let her own momentum carry her up and over. The grass would pad some of her fall, but Nelly hoped the woman would have the breath knocked out of her. While the woman was flat on her back, Nelly figured she could explain the error of ways to her.

However, when the woman was within arm's length, she raised her fist, aiming for Nelly's head. Nelly's anger blossomed into delight. She was especially fond of the arm drag take down. Just as the woman moved close enough to make contact, Nelly caught the arm aimed at her head. As she moved to one side, out of the woman's way, she twisted the woman's wrist with one hand and grabbed her shoulder with her other hand. By pushing all of her own weight on the woman's wrist and shoulder, she forced her to tumble face first into the lawn.

On a person not accustomed to the pain produced by an arm bar hold, it usually turned into a submission hold. And that's what Nelly wanted. This big island aristocrat to submit. But no sooner had the woman tumbled to the ground, she started trying to jerk her arm out of Nelly's grasp. If the woman succeeded in getting back to her feet, Nelly worried that she might get optimistic about her chances of winning. At least optimistic enough to start yelling for the neighbors. Nelly bent the woman's arm behind her back and slid around to her side so she could use her knee to push the woman back down to the ground.

As the woman's cheek sank back into the grass, Nelly leaned closer to her ear and asked, "Got any more gourds you want to throw?"

"Who's your family, Miss Pedicab?" The woman tried to get her knees under her for leverage.

Nelly sat down on the woman. "No family, Miss Hula. But you can call me Nasty Nelly the Cherokee Banshee."

The woman went limp. Soon, she raised her head, gazed into the distance, then tried to twist around to look at Nelly. "Cherokee?"

"Oh, not the way you're Hawaiian." Nelly eased the pressure off of the woman's arm, but kept sitting on her. Her anger had turned clammy. And now she was aware of the flesh she had been twisting, the woman underneath her.

"Then you're not really Cherokee?" The woman propped herself up on her other elbow.

"As far as I know, I'm more banshee that Cherokee." Nelly dropped the woman's arm and got off her. She knelt by her side.

Kaahumanu rolled over on her side and shook the arm Nelly had been twisting. "I agree with you there."

Nelly helped Kaahumanu to her feet. "I got out of professional wrestling because it encouraged me to do what I just did."

Kaahumanu brushed off the front of her dress. "I'm afraid I was asking for it."

"Screaming for it." Nelly walked to her pedicab and picked up the small gourd and the two pieces of the one she had broken.

"Keep that one for my apology." Kaahumanu pointed to the smaller gourd. "I'll take these pieces to remind me of what you did to my pride."

"You ought to make me pay for that." Nelly wondered what the going price was for a double gourd.

"No. It was my fault." Kaahumanu waved the broken gourd in front of her. A few seeds still whispered around inside. "But when I saw you with your beautiful hands and feet, selling yourself to strangers, I felt coals in my belly. 'Here I am,

' I said to myself. 'Trying to put together a hula festival with not enough dancers to fill out the show, and there's a perfect Hawaiian dancer with her rump in the air for people too lazy to walk the length of Waikiki.'"

"Looks like we both need to calm down." Nelly turned the gourd in her hands and felt the seeds sliding around like a small line of foamy surf.

"If you're not certain you're Cherokee, then you *might* be Hawaiian." Kaahumanu tapped the gourd in Nelly's hands. "Maybe the islands called to you, to have you come home."

"I don't see how I could be part of island life when I've enjoyed being violent for five long years."

Kaahumanu's laugh was deep and resonant as a lava tube. She pointed toward Diamond Head. "Don't you realize that volcanoes birthed these islands?"

For the first time since she'd arrived, Nelly felt the breeze cooling her down to the island's temperature. The Trade Winds calming her. Claiming her.

About the Author

Donald Secreast was born in Lenoir, North Carolina—a town that referred to itself for many years as the furniture capital of the South. Growing up in a town whose main industry was furniture manufacturing and spending some of his formative years working in several of those factories, it isn't surprising that his first story collection, *The Rat Becomes Light*, concentrated on the lives of the people who worked in those factories.

Desiring to learn as much about fiction writing as he could, Secreast pursued an MA in English from Appalachian State University. Soon realizing that he needed to learn more in particular about fiction writing, he attended the Writing Seminars at Johns Hopkins University where he studied with John Barth and Edmund White. After four years of teaching, Secreast still felt the need to receive more formal instruction in fiction writing, so he attended the Writers' Workshop at the University of Iowa, where he studied with Lynne Sharon Schwartz and James Alan McPherson. After a few more years of teaching, Secreast returned to the University of Iowa where, after four years, he received his Ph.D. in Modern British

Literature (1900-1945). During this second time at the University of Iowa, he published in 1990 that first short story collection, The Rat Becomes Light, which was the first book in a two-book contract with HarperCollins. His second collection came out in 1993, entitled *White Trash, Red Velvet*.

In 1992, Secreast began teaching at Radford University where he taught fiction writing and American Literature. After twenty-five years of teaching at Radford University, Donald Secreast has retired to Bristol, Virginia, where he has spent the first year of his free time traveling in Nevada, California, and Arizona with his painterly wife, Dianne LaForge. At home, he has been learning to garden, catching up on Scandinavian detective series, and working his way to being the writer he always hoped to be. In the back of his mind, he often hears the words of Pablo Neruda: "Cada dia, una muerta pequena."